BLUECOAT RENEGADE

Lieutenant Chadwick Stanton is based at Fort Leavenworth in Kansas. His over-extravagant lifestyle causes him to initiate a robbery of the regimental payroll, but blame is placed squarely on his envied and hated rival, fellow officer, Captain Bentley Wallace. The trial, a foregone conclusion, results in the shamed officer being drummed out of the service. Now Ben wants retribution. But Stanton, in a cataclysmic showdown in a remote Wyoming canyon, is determined to thwart him. Can Ben find justice?

DALE GRAHAM

BLUECOAT RENEGADE

Complete and Unabridged

LINFORD
Leicester

First published in Great Britain in 2007 by
Robert Hale Limited
London

First Linford Edition
published 2008
by arrangement with
Robert Hale Limited
London

British Library CIP Data

Graham, Dale
    Bluecoat renegade.—Large print ed.—
Linford western library
    1. Western stories
    2. Large type books
    I. Title
    823.9'14 [F]

ISBN 978–1–84782–166–9

Published by
F. A. Thorpe (Publishing)
Anstey, Leicestershire

Set by Words & Graphics Ltd.
Anstey, Leicestershire
Printed and bound in Great Britain by
T. J. International Ltd., Padstow, Cornwall

This book is printed on acid-free paper

1

Bad Apple

A blazing sun hung low over the desiccated parade ground of Fort Leavenworth, Kansas. Unrestrained by even the slightest hint of a breeze, the noonday heat had driven all but the most stalwart personnel inside the army post's adobe outbuildings.

Those who remained had little to say in the matter.

New recruits were being marched up and down the dusty square by a drill-sergeant who would have much preferred the dubious comforts offered by the fort's resident cathouse madam. Instead, he was having to wet-nurse kids who should have known better. Those gaudy recruiting posters had a lot to answer for. Bawling lustily at the sweating ranks, he had every intention of living up to his fearsome reputation and making their lives a misery.

A wry smile creased the angular visage of Lieutenant Chadwick Stanton. Seated in his favourite chair in the officers' mess, he nodded approvingly at the sergeant's vehement tones from over the rim of his third glass of five-star French brandy. That was one of the chief advantages of being an officer. You could delegate to the lower ranks, with no backchat. Just so long as the colonel didn't see. For if truth be known, Lieutenant Stanton should have been out there in the baking heat supervising the new intake.

At that moment he sensed a presence hovering on his right side.

Peering round, he gave the mess steward a weary look of disdain.

'You want something, Figgis?' he asked casually returning his gaze to the plodding display outside.

'A letter from the director, sir,' came back the rather hesitant response.

Stanton brushed an imaginary speck

of dirt from the rich blue of his tailor-made uniform. A curt flick of the wrist indicated for the epistle to be placed on the table alongside the brandy decanter.

Once the steward had departed Stanton offered the brown envelope a caustic frown. This was the third such item in as many weeks. The others had gone into the trash bin without so much as a glance. Stanton knew what they were.

Mess bills. The bane of his life.

And they were not the only final demands he had received.

Only the previous day, a blunt stipulation had been made regarding payment for the Arab stallion he had purchased. A grey-and-white appaloosa, it was the finest piece of horseflesh on the post. And now that snivelling horse-trader had the gall to start charging him five per cent interest per week extra on top of the $500 he had paid for the animal.

Well, not exactly paid. Not yet anyway.

Stanton gave a lethargic shrug, once again considering the envelope. Rolling his eyeballs impatiently, he reached over and tore it open, then hauled out the white sheet inside. After reading the contents, his close-set beady eyes popped, a poignant match for the gaping mouth.

'Surely it can't be that much?'

Stanton's stunned exclamation drew sympathetic stares from other fellow-officers taking their ease. They all knew and appreciated the curse of having to meet mess bills. Though none could claim to have ever reached the dizzy heights of Chad Stanton's excesses. Most assumed he had private resources. A wealthy patron to fund his extravagant lifestyle.

If only they knew.

And according to this letter, Stanton's days of living the high life were well and truly numbered. Unless he could find upwards of $400 minimum within the next seven days, he would be forced to resign his commission in shame. Only those hounded out of the military for theft and cowardice were considered lower than an officer who failed to honour his debts.

Once again Stanton stared at the damning evidence that threatened to condemn him as a welsher, a perfidious defaulter.

It read:

For the immediate attention of Lieutenant Chadwick Stanton of the Third Infantry Regiment based at Fort Leavenworth, Kansas.

Sir, It is with great regret that I must inform you that unless substantial repayments of your mess bill are made within the next seven days, I will have no other recourse but to place the matter in the hands of the fort's commanding officer, Colonel Harvey Masters. You will be aware that any officer whose bill exceeds $300 must be referred to the colonel for his attention. As your own debt is now approaching $400, this procedure has become long overdue.

I await your response.

Harrison Sandwich, Captain, Director of Officers' Mess Accounting.

Stanton screwed the odious indictment into a tight ball and threw it away in disgust.

Seven days.

Chad Stanton's entire future now hung in the balance. Even his tailor was kicking off about a down payment for his new uniform. None of the rough, itchy serge for him, Stanton only ever sported the finest of cloth, bespoke to fit perfectly.

These were just three of his creditors who were threatening to go to the colonel.

How in hell's name was he going to make any impression on all this lot in seven days? Dependence on the miserly pay of a humble lieutenant was no answer.

If he had made captain as he had fully expected, things would have been different. He could have avoided all this palaver, or at least delayed the inevitable whilst he thought of something. But the colonel had effectively blocked that avenue.

And all this was on account of that skunk Wallace. It was all his blamed fault. A hot flush turned Stanton's sunken cheeks a violent puce at the notion of his rival's having gained the upper hand.

'Bastard!'

The fervent exclamation lurched out. There followed a rapid bout of coughing to hide the outburst. Nobody had noticed. Scowling into his brandy-glass, Stanton twirled the waxed ends of his moustache. It was a nervous twitch that signified inner turbulence and a desire for retribution.

Yes indeed, *Captain* Bentley Wallace, you have a lot to answer for.

Stanton's lip curled down in an ugly snarl. He was senior both in years and service, yet it was Wallace whom the colonel had decided to make up to captain.

Favouritism, that was what it was. Wallace had sucked up to the commanding officer and been rewarded accordingly. And all because of family ties, his father being a three-star general and war hero.

Stanton gave a blunt snort of derision.

Well, you won't get away with it, *Captain* Wallace. I'll cut you down to size and no mistake. Chad Stanton silently mouthed a lurid determination to avenge himself on his hated rival.

All he had to do now was figure out a means of achieving his devious ends.

Another couple of brandies and he had figured out the course that his revenge would take. He set down the glass beside the empty decanter and rose somewhat unsteadily to his feet. His dark eyes narrowed, a steely determination tightening the gaunt features of his angular face.

Once outside the stuffy confines of the mess, Stanton shrugged off the effects of his overindulgence like a rattler shedding its skin. Shoulders squared off, he set his kepi at a jaunty angle and headed back towards his quarters. For the visit he had in mind, ordinary range clothes were called for. It would not do for an infantry officer to be seen heading downtown and communing with the likes of Polkadot Charlie Muldoon.

★   ★   ★

An hour later, Stanton was knocking at the door of Muldoon's room. It was located on the second floor above the Prairie Dog saloon in downtown Leavenworth at the end of a dimly lit corridor. His eyes nervously flicked back along the grimy passage. This was not a liaison that he wanted to advertise.

Polkadot Charlie was known as a scheming n'er-do-well who would set his hand to all manner of skulduggery, provided of course the price was right. Intimidation, gun-running, duplicity and robbery were all his stock in trade. And on this particular occasion, it was the last of these skills that Stanton wished to exploit. When not engaged in any nefarious schemes, Muldoon held court in the saloon below as the Prairie Dog's resident gambler.

At the third knock a gruff voice punched through the thin wood of the door. Muldoon always liked to keep his visitors waiting. It gave him an edge, a feeling of supremacy.

'Come in then!' The blunt tone contained a calculated measure of irritation. 'If'n you have to.'

Muldoon was finishing off his lunch. Wiping the gravy from thin lips, he peered at his visitor from beneath bushy eyebrows that met in the middle. A skinny dude in his forties, Muldoon tipped his grey derby to the back of his skull-like head.

Wearing a trite smirk, he attempted to impart an aura of suave sophistication into his persona by sporting the garish vest that had given him his nickname. The Van Dyke beard, badly in need of a trim, was supposed to enhance the image. It failed miserably. He was nothing more than a hard-nosed thug in disguise. And no amount of fancy duds would change that.

Chad Stanton attempted to conceal his distaste at having to deal with such a repulsive character. Affecting a nonchalant air of disregard, he leaned casually against the door jamb.

But Muldoon was no fool. He knew what the army man was here for. Nothing within the environs of Fort Leavenworth and the bustling metropolis beyond the confines of the army post escaped his eagle eye for long.

'So what can I be doing for you, Lieutenant Stanton?' he asked, biting off the end of a long cheroot and lighting up. 'Couldn't by any chance have something to do with a certain Captain Wallace, could it?' Muldoon deliberately laid stress on the military rank, knowing that it would irk his guest.

The gambler's punchy remark brought a flush to Stanton's lean features. He bristled inwardly but held his cool, levelling a baleful eye on the pretentious dandy.

Ignoring the jibe, he said, 'I have a job for you.'

Muldoon puffed on his cigar, allowing a trickle of blue smoke to dribble from the thin line of a mouth before responding. Then he stroked his pointed beard thoughtfully.

Stanton was no stranger to either the Prairie Dog or its resident gambler. They had done business on previous occasions.

One incident had involved a soiled dove at the Palace Sporting Club, who had threatened to report Stanton to his commanding officer for 'excessive zeal' during one particularly ardent session in an upstairs boudoir. When she had refused to countenance some rather bizarre proclivities, the army man had left her in no fit state to ply her trade for upwards of a month thereafter.

Muldoon had persuaded the girl that it would be in her best interests to leave the fort at the earliest opportunity.

The second had involved the illicit sale of purloined whiskey to the Prairie Dog's proprietor. Stanton had been the officer in charge of regimental stores at the time. He had laid the blame for the missing liquor squarely on to the shoulders of the quartermaster sergeant. The poor dupe had been court-martialled. He had then suffered the humiliation of having his stripes ripped off in front of the entire garrison prior to being reduced to the ranks.

'It couldn't have anything to do with all those unpaid bills that keep falling into your lap, could it, Lieutenant?'

Stanton's jaw fell open. 'How do you know about that, Muldoon?' he snapped.

The gambler tapped his beaky snout knowingly and winked.

'Now that would be telling.'

'Got those grubby fingers of yours in a whole heap of pies, haven't you?'

The army man's acerbic jibe stiffened

the gambler's back.

He levelled an icy glower at his visitor. Then in a clipped voice he retorted, 'You've heard the saying, hear all, see all and say nothing! Well, that's my motto. Now spit your grief or eat dust. I'm busy.' He sat down with the intention of continuing his interrupted supper.

Stanton huffed and bridled at the notion that this scapegrace could be privy to all his financial dealings. But he needed the critter's help if he were to extricate himself from the tight spot he had got himself into, and come out on top.

'No need to get all fired up,' Stanton countered flippantly. 'Only joshing.'

Muldoon shrugged whilst forking a mouthful of stew into his mouth. The ball was in Stanton's court now as far as he was concerned.

'There'll be a hefty wad of green-backs coming your way,' pressed Stanton, taking a seat opposite the guzzling gambler. It was a struggle to conceal the abhorrence he felt for this odious creature. So he hurried on. 'You were right, of course. It is about Wallace. That promotion should have been mine.'

'Figured as much.' Muldoon smirked.

'This plan I've worked out will put the kibosh on that sneaking polecat and pay off my dues at the same time. Plus a little something left over to help me celebrate.' His hand reached out to grab Muldoon's arm. 'And we're not talking chicken-feed here. There's big bucks in this.' Stanton drew away, rising as if to leave. He gave a careless shrug of his narrow shoulders. 'Still. If you're not interested — '

'How much we talking about?' shot back the gambler.

Stanton resumed his seat, extracted a long Cuban cigar of his own and bit off the tip. He waited until he had lit up before continuing, knowing that he had Muldoon well and truly hooked.

'Could be upwards of five thousand in that safe.'

'You're wanting me to rob a safe?'

exclaimed the gambler, his eyebrows raised in startled disbelief.

'The regimental payroll will be arriving tomorrow.' Stanton puffed eagerly on the fine Havana, exhaling a trail of blue smoke. 'And Wallace is duty officer in charge. My plan is to slip a Mickey Finn into his coffee. Then it's up to you.'

Having regained his composure, Muldoon said, 'So what do you want me to do?'

'When I'm sure that Wallace is out cold for the night, I'll slip into his quarters and get the keys to the office and the safe. Be outside the window of my quarters so I can pass them down. The rest is up to you.'

'Couldn't this dude just claim he'd been drugged?' suggested Muldoon with a sceptical twist to his ugly mush. 'We'd have the dough, but your boy would still be in a job and mad as hell too.'

Stanton gave him a leery smirk.

'Not once I've finished with him.'

'Uh?'

'Whiskey, my card-dabbling friend.'

Stanton was now thoroughly enjoying himself. He could already envisage the shame that would be heaped on to his disgraced colleague, not to mention the surprised looks on the faces of his creditors as he paid them off with a nonchalant flourish.

A dreamy cast played across Stanton's face. Then there was the colonel — calling him into his office to offer him the vacant captain's post. He rubbed his hands in gleeful anticipation.

'What about it?' Muldoon snapped. He was clearly baffled, and becoming a mite impatient with this strutting peacock. 'Whiskey is for tipping down your throat as far as I'm concerned.'

'Exactly!' sniggered a preening Chad Stanton. 'And that bastard Wallace will be getting more than he bargained for. By the time I've finished with him, the whole of Leavenworth will know that he was drunk, completely pie-eyed, while on duty. And this one is not just

17

any old duty. Guarding the regimental payroll is a responsibility that affects every man on the post.' A mirthless cackle erupted from between pursed lips. 'After losing that he'll be lucky to escape with only being cashiered. The colonel might even stick him in the poky.'

Muldoon was thinking hard. His quick gambler's brain was working overtime.

'Can't do a job like this on my ownsome,' he muttered, eyebrows twitching to emphasize the danger involved. 'I'll need to get me some help. Robbing an army pay-office is no simple undertaking. If we get caught — '

'With Wallace out of the way, it'll be plain sailing,' interrupted Stanton.

'All the same, I'll be wanting a bigger cut than usual.' Muldoon squared his shoulders, screwing his visitor with a hard gaze, challenging him to argue the point.

'Of course, of course, goes without saying,' blustered Stanton. They had now reached the crux of the matter. 'I'll give you a quarter of the take. Now that's a generous offer, isn't it?'

'Fifty-fifty or the deal's off,' shot back the gambler bluntly and without pre-amble.

'What?' ranted the stunned army officer. This new development had him nonplussed. 'I could get a dozen wharf rats like you to do this for a couple of bottles of hooch.'

'But they ain't gotten the brains, nor the guile of Charlie Muldoon.' Casually straightening his cravat, the gambler aimed a lurid smirk at the other man. 'Nor the information! It would be a pity if the colonel were to find out that one of his prized young officers was nothing but a thief and a swindler.'

'Why, you gutless varmint.'

Stanton's hand fell to the holstered revolver on his hip. But before he could draw it, the hard barrel of a tiny twin-barrelled Deringer jabbed into his ribs. Muldoon had preempted the move. A good gambler always thinks two steps ahead. A tight scowl lent his skeletal visage a ghoulish appearance in the half-light cast by the single lantern.

Stanton shivered involuntarily.

'Fifty-fifty, right down the middle,' Muldoon repeated flatly whilst maintaining his cool. 'Or the deal's off. And your goose will be well and truly cooked.' The poker-face remained even and blank, the small gun firmly insistent. 'So what's it to be, Lieutenant Stanton . . . sir. Are we in or out?'

The army officer knew he had been outsmarted. He had no choice but to accept.

'Just make sure this goes off without a hitch,' he growled acidly, trying to regain lost ground.

The gambler relaxed, slowly and purposefully returning the Deringer to his vest pocket. 'Have I ever let you down before?'

The next hour was spent refining the plan.

To help placate the fuming officer, Muldoon sent down to the bar for a bottle of champagne to seal the bargain.

'On me, of course,' he enthused with a oily smirk, knowing full well he had got far more than he had any right to expect.

2

Night Callers

Lieutenant Stanton was sweating. He was secreted in a broom cupboard almost opposite the closed door of his detested adversary's room in A Wing where the cavalry officers had their quarters. All the muscles in his skeletal frame were stretched to fever-pitch. A shuffling at the far end of the corridor made his hair stand on end. It was the arrival of the mess steward.

Chad Stanton knew that his adversary was a stickler for routine. And the aspect of this that interested him most was the fact that Ben Wallace always had a pot of coffee sent up from the mess before going on duty. The steward placed the tray on a table outside Wallace's door, then knocked to announce the delivery. He waited for a muted acknowledgement before departing.

This was Stanton's chance — his one and only opportunity if the treacherous piece of skulduggery he had devised was to be enacted tonight.

And he would have to be double quick. There was no telling when Wallace would deign to appear. One second or one minute — this was the moment when his fate was in the lap of the gods.

Displaying the agility of a mountain cat, Stanton whipped open the cupboard door and darted over to the tray. The all-important knock-out drops in the tiny glass phial were clutched between thumb and forefinger. Ears attuned to every nuance of sound, he silently removed the coffee-pot lid and tipped the contents into the steaming brown liquid. A brief swish to disperse the potent draught, then he slipped back into his hidy-hole.

He barely had time to draw breath before Wallace opened the door. Stanton tensed. Only when the door closed again did he emit a deep sigh of relief. A wry smile played across his gaunt features, revealing white teeth that gleamed maliciously in the dim light. He hooked a solid gold pocket watch from his tunic pocket and glanced at the time.

It read 9.35 p.m.

In normal circumstances, Wallace would be at his post in the payroll office by ten o'clock. Stanton reckoned he needed to wait a further ten minutes after that before he could execute the next phase of his plan. By then, the Mickey Finn should have played its own vital role in the proceedings.

That period of enforced incarceration in the cloying darkness of the tiny cupboard dragged by with oppressive slowness. Each minute seemed like an hour. There were a couple of anxious moments when other officers passed down the corridor before Stanton judged it time to emerge from his restricting bolt-hole. Globules of moisture dripped from the end of his angular snout.

Another glance at the watch told him it was 10.10 p.m.

The payroll orderly, a Sergeant Bowman, would be getting edgy, wondering anxiously what was keeping the duty officer. But he was unlikely to do anything for another half-hour.

Stanton cast a wary peeper along the corridor, listened carefully, then slipped into Wallace's room. The guy was laid out on the floor, dead to the world.

Stanton's lips drew back in a malevolent grin.

'This is where you get your just deserts, *Captain* Wallace,' he snarled aiming a vicious boot into the ribs of the comatose officer. There was no reaction. 'Being the son of a three-star general isn't going to save you this time. They'll throw the book at you after tonight's little episode.' Another brutal kick followed the first before Stanton realized that he needed to move fast.

After lifting the supine body into a chair, he removed a bottle of whiskey from a bag and proceeded to dribble the contents into Wallace's mouth. A liberal dousing of his uniform added to the intended illusion. The denouement was provided by the almost empty bottle clutched to his chest.

'If the top brass don't kick you out after this,' Stanton murmured half to himself, 'I'll resign my commission.'

All he needed now were the keys to the office and the safe containing the payroll. And there they were, lying next to Wallace's sword. He grabbed them up and moved over to the door. He had his hand on the knob, and was just about to step into the corridor when two chattering officers strolled past. They were discussing a wage-rise due to be paid out the follow day.

Although it had been a close call, Stanton couldn't resist a silent chuckle. After waiting for the prattling duo to disappear, he cautiously opened the door. The corridor was empty. It took but a moment to leave via the back stairs and make a swift detour behind the stable block back to his own quarters in B Wing.

Outside, all was quiet. It was a sultry night. The flag of the Third Infantry Regiment hung limp in the fetid air. Only the lone howl of a coyote out on the prairie disturbed the air of tranquillity. And the moon had seen fit to offer its support to Stanton's pernicious scheme by disappearing behind a rolling cloud-bank.

Everything was going according to plan.

It was a struggle not to appear in a hurry. If seen, a man running would be remembered. He forced himself to maintain a steady yet purposeful tread. After what seemed a lifetime, he found himself entering his own room on the second floor of the block.

The thought nudged his brain that soon, all being well, he would be exchanging the spartan quarters of an infantry officer for the far more prestigious domain of the cavalry. Horse-soldiers had always enjoyed a far higher esteem than their foot-slogging colleagues, especially among the ladies. And *Captain* Chadwick Stanton would ensure that such a situation worked in his favour.

But first, he had to ensure that Muldoon and his bunch of thugs did their business. They should be waiting below outside the block. Stanton turned down the oil-lamp, scurried over to the window and hauled up the sash. Outside nothing moved. Where were they? Then he saw a furtive movement over to his left as four dark shapes flitted out from behind a hut.

'You're late!' The guttural rap came from the lips of Polkadot Charlie. 'Me and the boys figured you had chickened out.'

'Keep your voice down,' hissed Stanton. 'D'you want the whole camp to know what game we're playing?'

'So where have you been?'

'It took longer than I figured, making it look like Wallace had drunk himself into a stupor. I had to get rid of the coffee. Couldn't leave the evidence lying around for some inquisitive lawman to sniff out the truth.'

'OK, OK,' snapped Muldoon impatiently 'Have you got the keys?'

'Catch!' said Stanton, dropping them out of the window. 'And remember. The next time we meet up it will be to split the proceeds.'

'Right down the middle,' cackled Muldoon.

'Yeah, yeah! Fifty-fifty,' rapped Stanton impatiently, injecting a mordant tone into the snap. 'Just make certain you don't bungle the job.'

'Like takin' candy from a baby,' scoffed the gambler. 'I'll see you back at my place in one hour.' Without another word, he and his three shadowy cohorts vanished like a puff of smoke, swallowed up by the blanket of darkness.

Stanton called after the disappearing figures with the panicky warning not to harm the orderly when they busted through the payroll-office door. The only reply was a macabre chuckle instantly whisked away by a stiff wind that had blown in off the prairie.

Quickly he closed the window, an uneasy knot lodging in the pit of his stomach. He didn't trust Muldoon, but there was nothing he could do about that now. Except wait, and pray. A sardonic twist of the lip spoke of the mocking irony of such a notion.

★   ★   ★

'Check your hardware!'

The throaty command issued from between tight lips as Polkadot Charlie drew to a halt behind the payroll office. They had made a circuitous route to reach their objective, taking full advantage of all the shadowy alleys and recesses within the confines of the fort. A cloudy night helped. But Muldoon wasn't taking any chances. With the amount of dough at stake, he had no desire to run into any unforeseen patrols that might well be at large.

Leavenworth was more than just an army base. It was the principal military prison for the whole of Kansas. In the decade prior to the Civil War, the town itself had become a major focus for the gathering of freight and pioneers on the edge of the frontier. Since then it had outgrown the original base to become a thriving metropolis in its own right.

'How much dough are we lookin' at here?' enquired a bulky, thick-set jigger by the name of Bull Ferris. 'Must be a hefty wedge tucked away in that safe.'

Muldoon grunted. He had no intention of revealing the exact amount to hired underlings. They were being paid for doing a job, and that was all.

'That ain't no concern of your'n, Ferris,' rapped Muldoon tersely. 'Just make sure to do as you're told, and nothing more.' His flinty gaze held the Bull in a withering glare. 'You're getting paid, ain't yuh?'

Ferris shrugged. 'Just askin', is all.'

'Well don't!' Muldoon snapped back. 'Now all of you, check them shooters. And no more smart-ass comments.'

The click of drawn hammers was

followed by a ratcheting of spun revolver cylinders as the robbers ensured their firearms were fully loaded. The discordant yammer sounded like a dozen firecrackers exploding. Muldoon's nerves crackled.

'And each of you is totin' a knife, right?'

Three blades instantly appeared, the silvery metal gleaming with deadly menace.

Muldoon gave a satisfied grunt.

'No shootin' unless the job goes badly and we have to make a run for it. Then it's every man for hisself.'

'You look after the horses round the back, Kid,' he said addressing a mean-eyed youngster. 'And keep an eye open for any patrols.'

'What should I do if 'n some one happens along?'

'Anything,' Muldoon rasped irritably, 'Use what little brain power there is under that carrot head.' The kid looked at him blank-faced. He was not the sharpest knife in the drawer. Muldoon lifted his eyes to the night sky in exasperation, then spluttered out, 'Bang that nice shiny pistol you're always twiddlin' round your finger on the wall to warn us. And keep out of sight. Got that?'

'Sure thing, Charlie.' Any implied sarcasm was lost on the young tearaway.

Muldoon looked stonily at the other two members of his crew.

'Anyone else got a problem?' Nobody answered. 'Right then. This is how we play it.' His next remark was to Bull Ferris. 'You go round the front. Make certain the coast is clear, then douse the lights. Me and Dutch Henry will follow you. As soon as I've unlocked the front door with the key, we dash in and get the drop on the orderly.'

Muldoon levelled a bleak eye on each of them in turn.

'*Comprendes?*'

This time they all nodded. The time for action had arrived. Nerves were keyed up, muscles taut as bowstrings.

Cocked pistol gripped tightly in his hand, Muldoon waited for Bull Ferris to turn down the oil-lamps, then hustled round to the front of the office. Sticking his ear to the door he listened carefully. A greasy smirk lit up his beady eyes. Stanton had been right. This particular orderly was prone to sleeping on the job. Even through the thick oak planking he could clearly hear the rumbling snores.

Silently he inserted the key in the lock and turned it. A brief click as the tumbler dropped. Then he slammed the door open and leapt inside.

The orderly was splayed out in a chair. He might have been prone to a touch of shut-eye on night duty but, like most soldiers, he could raise himself to instant alertness when the need arose. And he was rapidly arriving at the conclusion that this was just such an occasion.

Sergeant Thomas Bowman was an Indian-fighter of the old school, used to catnapping with one eye open. He had been given the job of payroll orderly due to his advancing years and declining eyesight.

But there was nothing wrong with his reflexes.

At the very moment the intruders careered into the office, he was awake. An eagle eye sought out the rifle propped against the desk. It was only six feet away. He lunged out of the chair, reaching a hand towards the weapon.

Dutch Henry's astute brain instantly assessed the situation. Deftly flicking the Smith & Wesson .44 to his left hand, his empty right reached across his body and palmed the sheathed Bowie on his left hip. In a single fluid movement, the glinting steel flew across the intervening space and buried itself up to the hilt in Bowman's neck.

The soldier had his hand around the stock of the Springfield rifle and had even managed to cock it. But that was as far as he got before the ten-inch blade cut his life short. A red fountain spurted from a severed artery as the man crumpled. A thick pool of blood quickly spread like the plague, seeping through cracks in the wooden floor.

The whole incident had happened in the blink of an eye.

Muldoon had known about the Dutchman's prowess with a knife, but this was the first time he had witnessed the guy's skill at first hand.

'That was some trick, Henry,' he gasped in stunned amazement.

'No trick,' muttered the heavy-set Dutchman. Retrieving the bloody weapon, he wiped the long blade on the orderly's trousers and sheathed it. 'Henry van der Bilk learn his art from father. Before coming to America, he did knife-throwing act in Amsterdam circus.'

'Tell me about it sometime,' said Muldoon, moving across to the safe. 'But first we gotta empty this safe of all them lovely greenbacks. Then we split the breeze before the hourly watch comes a-pokin' their snouts in the trough. Keep a look-out, Bull.'

The bruiser moved across to a window.

It took ten minutes to fill a pair of

saddle-bags with the banded packs of dollar bills.

'All finished here,' announced Muldoon, moving catlike across to the door.

'Hold it!' snapped Ferris, raising his arm.

'What is it?'

'There a soldier boy lookin' over here.'

'The guard patrol ain't due for another forty-five minutes,' railed Muldoon, wiping the sweat from his brow. 'I planned this set-up that way to give us time to skedaddle.'

'It ain't a patrol,' Ferris shot back. There was more than a hint of unease in his harsh tone. 'Just one man. But he's headin' right this way.'

'Must have wondered why no light on outside,' spat Henry. 'We should have left it on.'

'Too late fer that now,' hissed Muldoon. 'Get behind the door. I'll distract his attention when he comes in while you see to him.'

Just in time, the Dutchman leapt out of sight as the inquisitive trooper knocked on the door.

'You in there, Sergeant Bowman,' called out a tremulous voice.

Silence prevailed, broken only by the pounding hearts of the three robbers.

'Sergeant?' came the repeated summons now louder and more panic-stricken. 'Answer me, please. Is everything all right?'

Inside the office, Muldoon's heart was beating like a steam-hammer. He willed the soldier to enter the office. But the guy was clearly suspicious. He had stepped back, away from the open door. Any second now he was going to suss out the truth and call for the guard. Then they would have to shoot their way out. And with 200 troopers within easy reach, their chances of escaping were equal to those of a snowflake in hell.

Still Muldoon waited, nerve-ends screaming at fever-pitch as he prayed for a miracle.

And that must have been what happened.

Outside on the veranda a dull thud cut through the oppressive silence. Muldoon and the Dutchman frowned quizzically at each other.

Then, instead of the army trooper, pushing open the door to the office, it was the lanky red mane of Kid Striker that cautiously appeared.

Henry van der Bilk almost lost his balance as he tumbled forward, the wicked Bowie a whisker away from burying itself in the Kid's head. He grabbed a hold of the door-jamb to keep his balance.

'What in hell's teeth you playin' at, Kid?' he spluttered in a harsh Dutch brogue. 'I almost had you pinned to wall.'

Before any of the others could recover from the startling intrusion, a hard query cut through the nail-biting atmosphere.

'Where's that bluebottle, then?'

It was Muldoon who voiced their disquiet.

Striker sucked in a lungful of oxygen

before launching into his story.

'I was round the back lookin' after the nags when I saw this feller sauntering across the parade-ground. He was headin' for the barracks. I figured he must have just come off duty and was after gettin' some shut-eye.'

'Just get to the point!' interjected Muldoon with obvious irritation. 'We ain't got all night.'

'Y-yeah, s-sure thing, Polkadot,' stammered the Kid shuffling his feet. 'Just let me catch my breath.' He ogled the long knife sticking out of the wall by his head suddenly realizing just how close he had come to cashing in his chips. Hands shaking like a belly-dancer's midriff, Striker lit up a cigar and drew the smoke deep into his lungs. He needed the sharp bite to calm his jangled nerves before continuing.

'The guy stopped in mid-stride as if he was thinking. Then he started to head this way. When there was no answer to his call, he drew a pistol. He was gonna bust right in!' The Kid's voice had risen to a warbling treble. 'Probably reckoned to find out if his wages were still intact. I crept along the side of the office and peeped round the corner. The guy was on the veranda and about to step inside. That's when he stopped and turned away.'

'He musta figured it made more sense to raise the alarm,' commented Muldoon. Striker nodded. He was breathing heavily as he relived the jittery scene.

'Go on, Kid,' urged Bull Ferris, his gaze fixed wide-eyed on the youngster.

'That's when I knew that it was up to me to nobble his plans.'

'So you stuck him?' pressed Ferris.

The Kid nodded. 'First time I ever killed a man with a knife.' His eyes had a hunted look about them, the skin around them drawn waxy tight with suppressed anxiety. Again his lithe torso shivered involuntarily. 'It sure ain't like doin' it with a gun.'

'You done well, Kid.' Van der Bilk rested a comforting hand on his shoulder. There was a new-found respect in the Dutchman's tone. 'And you are right. It ain't easy using cold steel. Seeing your victim snuffing out his life up close.'

Ever the pragmatist, it was Muldoon who brought them back to the reality of their hazardous situation.

'Enough of this crap,' he snapped acidly. His next remark was to Ferris. 'Drag that sucker in here,' he ordered. 'The last thing we need is another meddlin' soldier boy to happen along and spot one of his buddies takin' a nap.'

Meanwhile, Dutch Henry had turned the office coal-oil-lamp down to no more than a faint glimmer.

'Time we weren't here,' announced Muldoon, swinging the pair of heavy saddle-bags over his shoulders. He threw the office keys to Striker. 'Lock up after us, then get rid of them keys in the nearest water-trough. You earned your spurs tonight, Kid.' The unexpected compliment perked up the young hoodlum. It was a rare display of emotion from Polkadot Muldoon. 'No sense in makin' it easy for them bluebellies.'

Outside, Muldoon scanned the immediate vicinity and the surrounding shadows for any sign of movement. Only a wandering hunk of tumbleweed chose that moment to scuttle across the parade ground. In the distance a dog howled at the newly emergent moon.

Satisfied, Muldoon led the way behind the payroll office where the patient horses were waiting. On foot, he led his men quietly in single file behind some adjoining buildings before mounting up.

Soon they were jogging away from the grim scene. With each passing minute, the tension manifestly eased for the quartet of robbers. No alarm had been raised.

Muldoon flicked open the lid of his watch and squinted at the dial in the half-light. 10.42 p.m. All being well, the hourly guard patrol would not discover the robbery for another quarter-hour giving them ample time to get back to the safety of the Prairie Dog saloon.

He afforded himself a smile of satisfaction. This had been a good job, well executed. Two men might have been killed in the process, but that was a chance you had to take for the rewards on offer. And there was no evidence to connect him or his men with the robbery.

Only that poor sap, Ben Wallace. He would be lucky to escape a hefty spell in the hoosegow after this.

But Muldoon's progress had not gone unnoticed.

Chad Stanton stuck his head out from behind a nearby wall. An infuriated scowl crushed the handsome features. There was not supposed to have been any lethal violence during the robbery. And he had no way of ascertaining the condition of Sergeant Bowman until the hourly patrol arrived and raised the alarm.

Still, he mused thoughtfully. Apart

from that, everything had gone according to plan.

Stanton could live with a couple of terminations so long as his debts could be paid off with a handsome profit to boot. Ridding himself of that asshole, Wallace, soon brought the colour back to his lean features.

3

Court-Martialled

Ben Wallace could barely comprehend what had happened to him. The week following his arrest had been a living nightmare. Being confined to barracks under house-arrest in the military prison attached to Fort Leavenworth was bad enough. But then finding himself accused of being drunk on duty and directly responsible for the robbery still left him completely baffled.

He knew that he had not touched a drop that night, not even a sherry after dinner in the mess. The duty of having to guard the fort's payroll had rested heavily on his shoulders. And Ben Wallace had always taken his responsibilities seriously.

For the umpteenth time he went over the events of that fateful evening. After dinner he had retired to his room to prepare for his night-shift at the payroll office. A mess orderly had delivered his regular coffee.

And that was the last he remembered.

The next thing, he was being man-handled out of his room to be marched directly across to his present quarters. As an officer, he had been accorded the dubious privilege of quarters that were more commodious than those of the ranks. Even so, they were meagre in the extreme.

It was not until the next morning, when he received a visit from the adjutant, the full meaning of the bizarre occurrence was revealed to him in all its gruesome detail. No amount of denial regarding the charges cut any ice with the grim-faced senior officer. As far as Major Stonegate was concerned, the evidence spoke for itself. He had even suggested that Wallace was likely to be charged with aiding and abetting the robbery, including the murder of two troopers.

Wallace knew he had been set up, framed. But who would want to pull such a heinous stunt? He shook his head in despair. It was clearly aimed at keeping him out of the way while the payroll was stolen. It had worked perfectly. And there was nothing he could do to prove his innocence. He had been caught having drunk himself unconscious, the damning evidence clutched in his hands.

The robbers had got clean away with a month's wages. All the military hierarchy could do was hope that the county sheriff would apprehend the perpetrators. Until that occurred, at least they had a scapegoat. And they had every intention of making a prime example of him.

The regiment was in no mood for clemency. Their wages had been stolen, two comrades brutally slain. Some one had to pay. And that someone was clearly going to be Captain Bentley Wallace.

A week ago, Ben's future had looked

rosy. The young cavalry officer seemed destined for great things. He had come through the military academy at West Point with flying colours. Not only had Second Lieutenant Wallace achieved the accolade of being selected as the most promising cadet of his intake, he had gained the highest ever overall grades in all his courses.

His appointment as officer commanding Two Company of the Third Cavalry attached to Fort Leavenworth was his second appointment. It had only taken him six months to gain a full captaincy.

And within the military households attached to the fort, the handsome young officer had been considered a fine catch, an eligible bachelor to be pursued and hogtied. Numerous wives of the senior ranking officers at Leavenworth had encouraged their daughters to make his acquaintance with a serious view to just such an entrapment. The fact that Ben was the son of renowned Civil War hero,

General Harvey Wallace, clearly had no influence on these fervent aspirations!

All that was now a mirage, a pipe dream. Ben opened his bloodshot eyes and peered around at the bare walls of his prison. His mother had called to see him the previous day. It had been an embarrassing interlude. All that seemed to concern her was the shame, the disgrace that his thoughtless actions would bring on the family.

'This will not help your father's campaign to become the state governor, Bentley,' she asserted vehemently, pacing up and down the small room. 'How could you be so stupid?' Not waiting for, nor concerned with, a response, she hurried on: 'It's even been suggested that you were a party to the robbery.'

At this unwarranted assault on his integrity, Ben felt compelled to protest. He jumped out of his seat, anxious to defend himself. During his time in the military he had accepted his mother's need to maintain a social standing with the other wives. But he had thought she would at least show some concern, a spark of understanding for his predicament. A belief in his innocence.

He was clearly wrong. All she cared about was her status, her reputation in the community.

'And you're ready to believe them, aren't you, Mother?' The retort was uttered in a barely controlled manner. 'This has been a set-up from start to finish. Somebody has framed me.' His blue eyes narrowed to thin slits, as hard as flint. His next remark emerged as a rasping cut. 'And if I ever catch the scurvy polecat — '

The idle threat went unfinished as his mother interjected.

'How can you deny that you were drunk on duty?' she queried stuffily. 'The evidence is undeniable. Your father and I will never live this down. We will be forced to leave Leavenworth once your disgrace becomes common knowledge. How could you be so thoughtless?'

At this she burst into tears.

Ben Wallace turned away to hide a scornful grimace. What was the point in denying it. She would never believe him. Even so, the maternal condemnation had shaken him to the core. And he was sure that his father would be of a like mind.

'There's nothing more to be said then,' he muttered, trying to hide the abject disappointment he felt. 'I think you had better leave, Mother.'

That was the last he saw of Gwendoline Wallace.

Her unquestioning assumption that he was guilty as charged was reflected by the court martial which took place a week later.

Three senior officers listened to the evidence during the two-day trial. Chaired by the fort's commandant, Colonel Harvey Masters, their grim faces remained stony throughout the hearing. The young subaltern assigned to defend Captain Wallace tried his best. But it was obvious from the start that he, like everyone else, assumed the prisoner was guilty. The trial, as far as Ben was concerned, was a farce from start to finish.

And he pulled no punches in voicing his opinion, thus ensuring that everybody knew what he thought of military justice.

It therefore came as no surprise to anyone, least of all the accused, when he was found guilty and sentenced to be dishonourably discharged from the service. Only because there was a lack of hard evidence to prove that Ben had been complicit in the robbery, plus the fact that he was the son of an eminent general, did the court stop short of passing a custodial sentence.

They did, however, stipulate that the shamed officer would be publicly discharged in front of the whole garrison. This was a punishment normally reserved for the rank and file. Disgraced officers were allowed the privilege of disappearing discreetly. Not so for Ben Wallace.

And Lieutenant Chad Stanton was

there to enjoy the proceedings.

Dawn had just broken. Streaks of burnt sienna cut across the eastern horizon as the sun rose above the outer walls of Fort Leavenworth. The entire garrison was on parade. Lined up and standing to attention, they were here to witness the ignominy of a previously respected and well-liked officer. It was a rare occasion, and one that most troopers present had never previously beheld.

A hum of expectation filtered through the ranks like a fine desert breeze.

Then the moment of truth arrived.

Ben Wallace, clad in full dress uniform, was led out between two guards. The solemn trio came to a halt in front of the regimental flagpole. All of a sudden the wind had stilled, as if awaiting the grim pronouncement from the commanding officer. The forlorn banner hung loosely in sorrow, or more probably shame.

Two buzzards perched aloft were squawking in gleeful anticipation.

An angry murmur rippled through the lines of parading soldiers. This was the skunk who had allowed their wages to be stolen. And there wouldn't be another payroll delivery for at least another month.

Colonel Masters raised his hand. Instantly, a heavy silence settled over the massed ranks. The senior officer, mounted on a white stallion, rode stiffly across the parade ground and reined to a halt before the condemned man. This was a signal for the two guards to step back.

Masters peered down at this once promising officer. In five years, he could have been in command of his own post. The colonel's heart was sad, his thoughts a confused amalgam of disappointment and fury. But none of this was overtly on view. All that was presented to the world was a stony glare, flat and even without any show of compassion. Disicipline had to be seen to be maintained.

Silence reigned as the parade waited.

Then the indictment was read out in a slow heavy monotone given all the more solemnity as a distant roll of thunder echoed across the western plains.

'Captain Bentley Wallace . . . ' Fort Leavenworth's stolid commandant began. He paused to gather his thoughts, eliciting a brief cough to conceal the nervous hesitancy that had invaded his normally rich baritone. It wasn't every day that an officer was court-martialled. Still less publicly drummed out of the service. Surveying the ranks of expectant faces, he sucked in a lungful of air before starting afresh.

'Captain Bentley Wallace, you have this day been found guilty of gross professional misconduct and neglect of duty. Your heinous action, the result of an excessive consumption of alcohol, has allowed the success of a most serious robbery which resulted in the misappropriation of regimental funds.'

The colonel looked up from the prepared address, his cold eyes appraising the numerous twisted expressions that stared angrily back at him from the ranks. Not once did his frosty countenance meet that of the haggard man standing before him.

Then he continued.

'Far more serious, however, is the fact that two serving troopers died as a result of your unpardonable conduct. There can be no place in the United States military for the perpetrator of such a dire transgression as yours.' Only now did Colonel Masters choose to acknowledge the condemned man's presence, spearing him with a glare of pure venom.

'You, sir, have not only brought disgrace upon your family, you have shamed the proud uniform you should have been honoured to wear. The safe was opened with your keys which in my book makes you an accessory. If it had been up to the court, you would have most definitely received a custodial sentence. It is only out of regard for your father's eminent position that you have been spared that ignominy.

'The court's decision, therefore, is that you receive a dishonourable discharge — sentence to be carried out forthwith.'

The colonel's next remark was aimed at the adjutant.

'Major Stonegate?'

The appointed officer saluted smartly and stepped briskly forward.

'Sir!' he bellowed.

'Do your duty!'

'Yes sir!'

Marching round to face the accused man, Major Stonegate slowly yet methodically began the humiliating ritual.

First, the epaulettes were ripped from Wallace's shoulders. There followed the brusque removal of each and every brass button on his tunic. Lastly, he held out his hand, levelling a regard of arrogant scorn at the disgraced officer.

Wallace knew what was expected. He stared back through eyes that lacked any sign of life. His drawn face, ashen and haunted, was that of a corpse. And that was how he felt. He just wanted the ground to open and swallow him up. But there was this one ritual left — the ultimate dishonour.

Slowly he withdrew his sword and handed it over. Stonegate meaningfully raised the weapon then snapped the blade cleanly across his upraised knee. The sound of the cracking steel echoed between the fort's adobe walls. He threw the broken weapon at Wallace's feet, then stepped aside.

It was the signal for the fort's main gate to be hauled open. At the same time, the drum-roll began. The facing rank of troopers parted, creating a ten-foot wide passage.

The corridor of shame!

Someone had brought Ben's saddled horse across from the stable. The reins were briskly pushed into his hand.

Silence reigned. But only for ten seconds as the true import of recent events was absorbed.

Then a hand jabbed into the shamed man's back, propelling him forward towards the open gate. It was the signal for a roar of insulting and scornful taunts to bombard the condemned man. This time, nobody intervened. Rotten eggs, tomatoes, and even stones were thrown.

One hit Ben squarely in the face, tearing a lump of flesh from his cheek. It brought the hunched figure back from the grave into the nightmarish reality of his position. Quickly, he mounted up and spurred along the narrow corridor of jeering bluecoats. The open gate seemed a thousand miles away.

He allowed the large bay mare its head.

Eventually, in effect less than half a minute, the jeering chorus was left behind, fading to a grumbling murmer of discordant voices. The stunned man, totally bewildered and feeling little more than an empty shell, was now a civilian, plain ordinary Ben Wallace.

With his head slumped on to his chest he nudged the bay down the shallow grade towards the town of Leavenworth.

4

Bad News Travels Fast

Even the junior officers had joined in the fervent harassing of the disgraced officer. All, that is, except for Lieutenant Stanton. He couldn't erase from his mind the vengeful look that he imagined Ben Wallace had given him as their eyes met, though only for the briefest of moments as the prisoner had been marched across the parade-ground. And it had only registered with Stanton in the last few minutes.

Did Wallace Know?

Had that piercing glint in his eye been the threat of retribution? The tremor of guilt rippled through his taut frame, but only for an instant.

There was no proof. It was his word against that of a disgraced ex-officer. Nonetheless, the notion sat heavily on

Chad Stanton's shoulders. Moving away from the excited throng, he quickly hustled across to the mess and his favourite seat overlooking the parade-ground. A bottle of five-star French brandy should help assuage his unease.

It didn't.

And Chad Stanton was rapidly coming to the conclusion that his arch-rival was like a painful and persistent abscess. And always would be until that cyst was lanced. The more he drank, the greater the supposed threat became. Until it hung like the sword of Damocles above his head.

Stanton scrambled to his feet and headed for the stables.

* * *

As daylight finally surrendered its grip to the darkness of night, Ben Wallace was becoming ever more belligerent, his manner obtuse and aggressive. He had steadily made the rounds of

Leavenworth's numerous drinking-parlours. If the demon drink had been the reason for his unfair dismissal from the army, then he might as well embrace it with open arms.

And after securing a room at one of Leavenworth's cheaper and more seedy lodging-houses, he had proceeded to well and truly drown his sorrows.

Ben reached into his coat pocket. His searching fingers fastened on to the last of his silver dollars. Following his exit in disgrace from Fort Leavenworth, he had not even received the statutory one month's pay. The robbery had seen to that. Most of the other officers had been forced to take out loans to tide them over. Luckily Ben had always been thrifty and still had some money saved up.

But that had quickly disappeared over the counters of a dozen saloons. He had now reached the Prairie Dog.

'Gimme another bottle!' The slurred demand was met with a tight shake of the head from the rotund barkeep.

'You've had more than enough, mister,' he said, arms crossed to indicate his firm resolve. 'Now go sleep it off.'

'I'll decide when I've had enough,' postulated the soused drinker, slamming a bunched fist on the bar top. 'Now hand over that bottle.'

The barman flicked an eye towards a pair of hardcases who were idly playing cards. Kid Striker and Bull Ferris threw an eye at the stumbling man at the bar, then pushed back their chairs and stood up. When not engaged in more shady enterprises, the duo acted as unofficial guardians of the Prairie Dog saloon.

Ferris motioned for his young sidekick to approach the drunk from the front to gain his attention. It was a ploy they had perfected on numerous occasions before.

'You heard the man,' rasped Striker spreading his legs wide for balance, his arms hanging loose yet coiled and ready for action. 'It's bedtime. So why not just leave peaceful like. You don't wanna cause no trouble, now do you?'

'And who the hell are you?' snapped Wallace, lurching around to face the newcomer. A sour twist of his curled lip told the Kid that this dude was not going to go quietly.

Striker shook his red thatch, clicking his tongue in a mocking show of derision.

'Now that ain't too smart, fella,' he jeered. ''Cos if'n you don't quit this berg pronto, I'll throw you out head first.'

Ben's face creased in drink-induced amusement. 'You and whose army?' The irony of the challenge was lost amidst the alcoholic stupor. Then, without any warning he slung a right cross at the Kid's jaw. In any other circumstances it might have connected and done some damage. But Ben Wallace was too inebriated, his reflexes were slow and laggard. Striker merely rocked back on his heels, allowing the potential haymaker to spin harmlessly by.

'That the best you can do?' chortled the cocky sprog. In the blink of an eye his revolver was palmed and laid brutally across the head of the tottering drunk.

Wallace grunted under the jolting impact and went down on to one knee. A trickle of blood slid down his face. His vision blurred as the stunning blow threatened to lay him low.

'Didn't need you after all, Bull,' preened Striker, jabbing the .44 into his victim's ear.

'Pity,' replied his beefy partner. 'I coulda done with some action.'

'Well, you can help me sling this turkey out of here.'

Together, they bundled the tottering form outside, heaving him off the sidewalk.

Like a sack of potatoes, Wallace tumbled into the muddy street. Spitting out a mouthful of brown sludge, he stumbled to his feet, swaying drunkenly. His blue serge jacket, now buttonless and besmirched, flapped idly. A few onlookers sniggered at the sorry spectacle of a once-respected army officer having been reduced to the lowly status of a town bum.

'And you better not come back if'n you know what's good for you,' shot Ferris, setting his hat straight as the pair of bruisers coolly returned to their unfinished card game.

That was the moment Chad Stanton chose to tie up his horse outside a hardware store a block south of the Prairie Dog. He had business with Polkadot Charlie Muldoon and did not want his presence to be noted. The unceremonious ejection of Ben Wallace from the saloon came as a rather disconcerting jolt.

The man was clearly liquored up. In such a state he could quite easily start shooting his mouth off. Most people would merely scoff, putting it down to the rantings of a sore loser, a disgraced bluebelly. On the other hand, others might listen.

And wonder.

Stanton could not afford to take that chance. That was the reason for his surreptitious visit to the Prairie Dog. And judging by what he had just witnessed, he was none too soon.

The sooner Wallace could be permanently removed from circulation the better. He hurried up the back stairs to make the necessary arrangements with Charlie Muldoon.

★ ★ ★

Ben awoke the next morning with a stinking headache. He peeped around at the spartan surroundings of the flop house in which he now found himself. A hammer pounded the inside of his skull. Struggling on to one elbow, he screwed up his bloodshot eyes against the harsh glare of the sun beaming in through the window. He was still fully dressed, but the caked mud on his clothes had dried. Although much of it had been transferred to the already soiled bed-sheets.

Ben groaned aloud.

How could his life have been reduced to this level? No money, no prospects, and a disgraced pariah — shunned by all except the dross of society.

He staggered over to the dresser and poured a bowl of water from the chipped pitcher. After liberally dousing his head half a dozen times in the tepid liquid, at least he was able to dispel the clinging remnants of the hangover. Perhaps now he could begin to think rationally and face up to what the future had in store for him.

First off, he needed a job. With his knowledge of the vast open territories west of the Missouri, he ought to be able to secure a scouting post with one of the freighting companies that operated out of Leavenworth. They were always looking for experienced hands to lead the supply trains down the Santa Fe Trail.

After cleaning himself up, Ben shucked out of the filthy bluecoat jacket in favour of a buckskin he had luckily retained as a spare in his saddle-bags. No sense in advertising his recent profession to potential employers.

Then he went down to the dining-hall to enjoy a hearty breakfast paid for with his last silver dollar. There was no knowing where his next meal would come from.

Ben's first call was at the Madison Freight Hauliers on Delaware Street. He paused inside the office door. The room was full of boxes and oddments of cargo waiting to be packed. Two men were arguing over a consignment invoice.

'That load needs to be on the trail by noon today,' announced an older man dressed in a smart blue suit. His tone was firm and countenanced no rebuttal as he puffed on a large Havana cigar. He was clearly the man in charge.

'No chance, Mr Salinger,' returned the second man with equal finality.

'Why not?' snapped Salinger.

'We're two drivers down with influenza.'

Salinger waved a hand aimlessly towards the rear of the building, 'Them wagons are scheduled for delivery in Santa Fe by early May at the latest. We're already a week late. Can't you hire some other men?' he persisted, the spherical face reddening with evident frustration.

'They've been off sick for three days so half the wagons ain't loaded.'

The second man was the same age but clad in working gear. Grizzled and under pressure, the foreman was sweating, trying desperately to keep his cool under the boss-man's caustic grilling.

That was when he noticed Ben standing by the door.

'You want something, mister?' he said firmly but politely. This guy could be a potential client.

'If it's a driver you want, then I'm your man,' Ben said, stepping forward, hat in hand.

The foreman's bushy eyebrows lifted. Hope registered in his gaze. Perhaps this was the lifeline he needed.

'You know the hauling business, then?' he asked.

'I can handle wagons,' said Ben confidently. 'And I know the territory from here to Santa Fe like the back of my hand. Every bend in the trail, likely spots for an ambush by road agents, and which tribes are causing trouble.'

The foreman nodded approvingly.

'Seems like just the kind of fella we need,' he said, addressing Salinger.

The bossman glowered from behind a pall of blue smoke. He was not convinced.

'What's your name?' he rapped.

'Ben Wallace.'

Salinger's back stiffened. His beady eyes narrowed adopting a frosty glare. Teeth bared in a taut rictus, he skewered the newcomer with a look of pure loathing.

'There ain't no work for you here,' he averred brusquely before turning away.

'But Mr Salinger,' pressed the confused foreman. 'We need — '

'I said we don't want him,' shouted Salinger, cutting him short. Then, in support of the abrupt rebuff, he hurried on, 'I need freighters with experience. Men I can trust.'

'What makes you think you can't trust me?' responded Ben caustically.

'Sorry, Mr Wallace.' The foreman shrugged contritely. 'The boss always has the final say.' He had no intention of going against his superior, valuing his own job too much. The two men continued their discussion as if Ben did not exist.

Outside, he frowned. Could they have heard about his discharge from the army. It seemed unlikely. Surely the news couldn't have spread through the commercial district of Leavenworth that quickly.

Unless someone had passed the word to give him the cold shoulder!

The next two haulage companies he tried appeared to corroborate his suspicions.

So when he eventually came to the

fourth, at the end of Shawnee Street down by the docks, Ben was getting hot under the collar. Mad as an angry sidewinder, he was not about to be fobbed off yet again. He was directed to the wagon boss round the back in the loading yard.

At first the guy was helpful, intimating that he could always use a good reliable hand. So once the preliminary enquiries had been passed and the proprietor asked for his name, Ben was ready. He immediately shot back with his own rejoinder.

'What does that matter?' he retorted bluntly, squaring up to the burly teamster. 'I'm up to the job. You said so yourself. So are you going to give it to me or not?'

The man stepped back a pace, scepticism clouding his dark, saturnine features. He eyed Ben from beneath heavy black brows.

'Seems to me that a feller who won't reveal his name has somethin' to hide.'

The two men stood there glowering

at each other. It was Ben who broke the tense silence.

'The name is Bentley Wallace,' he offered, injecting a taut passion into the name.

'Umph!' sneered the teamster. 'I figured as much. You're that skunk of a bluecoat what's just been kicked off the fort, ain't yer? A damn blasted disgrace to the uniform. Well I don't hire me thieves and low-lifes, especially those what'd steal from their own kind.' The man drew himself up to his full height. 'Now get off my property before I call the marshal.'

This was too much for Ben.

'Who's been spreading poison about me,' he snarled angrily.

'I'll take on whomever I choose,' replied the teamster known as Tom Fisk. 'And that don't include a rat like you.'

Ben's face purpled, assuming a lethal glower of pent-up frustration. Without warning he lunged at the man. Caught off guard, Fisk was jolted by the solid right-hander that connected with his jaw. He emitted a startled choke, staggering back against a wagon. But Tom Fisk was no weakling and quickly recovered. He shook his head and side-stepped as Ben made to deliver another blow.

Backing away, he called out. 'Hey! Frank, Barney! Over here quick! There's some crazy jackass tryin' to kill me.'

From the far side of the yard, two men appeared. They were tough-looking bruisers. Quickly taking in the situation, they hurried across the yard. One drew a pistol and aimed it in Ben's direction. He fired on the run and the shot went wide, ploughing into the ground some three feet to Ben's left. But it was near enough. The other man stopped to take a more careful bead on their boss's attacker.

Ben threw himself behind a large pile of boxes. And only just in time. Two more shots rang out. Splinters of wood flew in all directions, no more than two inches from his head. He ducked down as another shot plucked at the sleeve of his jacket.

As the lead began to fly, the haulage boss scrambled out of the firing-line to direct the action.

Unarmed, Ben cursed himself for allowing his quick-fire temper to take over. He should have just walked away. It was too late to cry over spilt milk now. He knew that to survive, a rapid exit from the freight yard was needed. These guys were hard-nosed river rats and not about to take any prisoners.

Luckily, they didn't know he was defenceless. Following their initial charge, the two heavies had taken cover behind a wagon.

Ben looked round to his rear. He was twenty yards from the back fence. And there was a gap in the rotting planks. That was his only way out of this situation. And there was no time to lose. The boss man had a side view of Ben's position denied to his underlings and was pressing them to finish him off.

'Circle round to the left, Frank,' he

urged vigorously. 'You take him from the right, Barney.'

Momentarily, the two men hesitated. They had no wish to run into a hail of bullets from their concealed adversary. The boss railed at them impotently to get a move on. Then he realized that his assailant must be unarmed as there had been no return fire.

'Shift yer asses,' he rapped. 'Ain't yer figured it out yet? The critter's wide open. He ain't got no weapon.'

Ben could perceive a shuffling of feet as his two attackers began what was in essence a simple pincer movement. If he didn't move now, he would be a dead man in less than a minute.

He grabbed hold of a box and heaved it over the top of the stack in Frank's direction. He could only hope that his aim was accurate. The answering howl of pain as the box connected was music to his ears. But this was no time for self-congratulations. Barney would be appearing round the other side at any second.

Bending low, Ben hurtled towards the fence gap. He had never run so fast, those twenty yards feeling like a hundred. As bullets flew past, he zigzagged frantically to present a more difficult target. Midway across, he stumbled, almost falling to the ground as a scorching bolt of lightning seared his left arm.

Barney had found the range.

'Yahooo!'

A crow of delight went up from the river rat.

But it was only a flesh wound. The next minute Ben was through the gap and sprinting round the corner of a nearby warehouse.

'Get that sneaky bastard,' rang out a spirited howl from the freight boss. By this time three other drivers had appeared in the yard. 'I'll pay a hundred-dollar bonus to the man who brings him back — dead or alive!'

Ben knew there was no way he could remain in Leavenworth a moment longer. The chase was on. And there would be a whole heap of riffraff after that reward. He thanked providence that behind the grand façade, the town was a warren of interconnecting alleyways enabling him to shake off his pursuers quickly. Following a tortuous detour, he was able to reach his lodgings without incident.

In less than half an hour, he was mounted and spurring his mount along one of the less frequented trails heading north-west along the left bank of the Missouri. His destination was the burgeoning town of Omaha. Ben figured it would take him five days of steady riding.

Nobody knew him in Nebraska, and Ben reckoned that he should easily be able to pick up a scouting job with one of the wagon trains heading west bound for Oregon and California.

It would have been quicker and easier to head in the opposite direction. Independence was nearer. But the army post there would surely by now have learned of his ignominious discharge.

And he was of the opinion that no amount of fervent denials as to his guilt would sway the military authorities.

A dark cloud enveloped the tanned features, turning the normally placid expression to one of implacable resolve. His avowed intention was that some day he would return to Leavenworth and prove his innocence. Of that he was determined.

But this was clearly not the time. He recalled the adage: *He who turns and runs away* . . . .' Many a coward had quoted this as an excuse for deserting the battlefield.

Ben Wallace knew he was no hero, but neither was he a spineless weakling. In the current circumstances, such a course of action made sense.

5

Bushwhacked

At about the same time that Ben Wallace was picking a course among the dwarf willows that festooned the river-bank beyond the town limits, Chad Stanton was hustling up the back stairs at the rear of the Prairie Dog saloon. He was anxious to learn how his plan to get rid of Wallace had fared.

Without bothering to announce his presence, the visitor barged straight into Polkadot Charlie's room. The gambler was studying some papers behind a large leather-topped desk. A smoky oil-lamp swung languidly, throwing the rest of the room into a haze of shadow.

Stunned surprise at this unwarranted intrusion registered on Muldoon's gaunt visage. But only for an instant. It was replaced by a scowling grimace.

'Hustling into a man's room without knocking ain't a healthy thing to do,' he snarled, pointing the small Deringer at Stanton's head. 'You're damn lucky I ain't the nervous kind, else you'd be a dead bluebelly by now, mister.'

Stanton shrugged off the warning impatiently.

'Did you fix Wallace?' he asked bluntly.

'Don't worry,' replied the gambler, slowly pocketing his tiny firearm. 'He won't be hangin' around this town for much longer.'

'What d'you mean?' Stanton frowned.

'I put the word out on him. Everybody knows what he did. There's no chance of him gettin' work here. None of the teamsters is gonna employ a discharged thief. Especially one that's an ex-cavalry officer.' Muldoon uttered a harsh chortle. 'The dude will be forced to leave town. That's the last we'll be seein' of him.'

Momentarily, a silence enveloped the room, heavy and sombre.

It was broken by the army man

slamming a balled fist down on the desk. A glass of whiskey leapt into the air, spilling its amber contents over the desk.

'You durned fool!' he roared, flecks of spittle burbling from between tightly clenched teeth. His angular face was purple with irritation. 'You were supposed to get rid of him permanent. And you know what that means.'

'You all right, boss?'

A third voice came from the open door, slicing through the tense atmosphere. It was Kid Striker. A .44 Colt Frontier was gripped firmly in his right hand and pointing unerringly at the back of Stanton's head.

Muldoon had jumped to his feet, lips drawn back in a livid glower of hostility. Now he smiled mirthlessly, relaxing as the odds once again swung in his favour.

He nodded, indicating for the young tearaway to lower his revolver.

'It'll cost you a sight more'n what you paid before if it's another killin' yer after,' scoffed Muldoon, pouring out two glasses of whiskey. With purposeful intent that was not lost on Stanton, he handed one to Striker. Both sipped their drinks whilst disdainfully eye-balling the army man.

'So what's it to be.' Muldoon leered.

Stanton knew they had him backed into a corner. Muldoon held all the aces.

'OK,' he said. 'But this time you do the job properly, right?'

Muldoon raised his hands in mock surrender.

'You're the paymaster, Lieutenant . . . sir.' He clicked his heels and offered Stanton an exaggerated salute. The latter struggled to maintain his dignity, his taut features resembling a fiery sunset.

Just then a grubby urchin appeared in the open doorway. He was breathing heavily.

'Got some'n for me, Weasel?' said Muldoon to the little sprout. The kid was one of numerous messengers whom Muldoon employed to keep him informed of the day-to-day happenings in Leavenworth.

'There's been a ruckus down at Tom Fisk's haulage yard.' The kid paused for breath. He had obviously run all the way up town from the docks.

'Go on,' urged Muldoon.

'Some guy didn't like bein' told there was no work for him. Cut up rough. Then scarpered when some of Fisk's drivers appeared and started loosing off with their guns.' The youngster stared at Muldoon, then hopefully thrust out a dirty mitt. 'Did I do well, Polkadot?' he asked eagerly.

Muldoon stroked his beard. considering the news. He knew that the kid had to be referring to Wallace.

'What happened to the guy?' he shot back.

'He lit out fast,' replied the kid, 'but one of the bullets nicked him.'

'Where'd he go?'

'Last I saw he was heading north along the back trail towards Atchison.'

Again the doe-eyed kid held out his paw. Muldoon dug into his pocket and extracted a half-dollar piece. He flicked the shiny coin up, the kid expertly snatched it out of the air. After quickly testing it with yellowed teeth, he disappeared.

'So now we know which way he's headed,' offered Striker.

Muldoon remained silent, thinking. He paced up and down the small office, a deep frown lacing his ribbed forehead. Neither Stanton nor the Kid interrupted. Eventually the gambler drew up his chair and sat down.

'This is the way I figure it,' he announced. 'Wallace is heading north. The nearest town likely to offer him work where they ain't likely to have heard about him is Omaha. A sharp rooster like that oughta have no trouble gettin' taken on by one of the wagon outfits headin' west.' Muldoon lit a cigar before continuing. He inhaled deeply, allowing the smoke to trickle from between pursed lips.

'So he'll have to stick to the back trails — at least for the next few days, to avoid bein' recognized. That's how we catch up with him. Me and the boys can take the main trail north along the east bank. We'll make better time. And it'll enable us to find some handy spot to waylay him. I reckon Nemaha Gap will be ideal.'

He smiled luridly at Stanton.

'That suit you, *Captain* Stanton?' Muldoon shared a wry smirk with his young sidekick. 'Promotion and all that goes with it oughta be worth say . . . ' He cocked an eye at the drab ochre ceiling '. . . say a thousand? Plus expenses, of course.'

Stanton's eyes popped. But what choice had he? None. He nodded, then swung on his heel and left.

'I figure that calls for another drink, don't you, Striker?'

The Kid nodded enthusiastically. Working for Polkadot Charlie Muldoon was proving to be quite a profitable enterprise for the young gunslinger.

* * *

Once the town limits of Leavenworth had been left behind Ben slowed his mount to a steady canter. He kept up a relentless pace until sundown, pausing only to relieve himself and give the horse time to get its second wind. A night camp was established well off the trail and out of sight.

For the next two days he avoided contact with all the settlements that hove into view by detouring around their fenced perimeters.

He was aware that news of the army's payroll loss and his untimely departure from Fort Leavenworth would have spread rapidly along the frontier grapevine. All the same, he felt that once he had put fifty miles between himself and the source of his infamy, he ought to be safe from the meting out of rough justice.

By the third day Ben was beginning to feel confident that he had escaped any reprisals. Now he was just another anonymous traveller bound for Nebraska.

Ahead of him a line of pine-clad hills ran east to west for a distance of fifty miles. The trail forked into the only gap in the abrupt escarpment at a point where the Big Nemaha River had carved out a deep ravine. On either side soaring cliffs overshadowed the narrow cutting.

This was the first line of hills that Ben had encountered in the otherwise level terrain. And he gave it no serious consideration. Only the fact that beyond the ten-mile gorge, when the land once again assumed the appearance of a billiard-table, he would have an easy run direct to Omaha.

★   ★   ★

'That him?'

It was Kid Striker who spoke up. It was his turn to stand watch. The others were reclining on the blind side of the rocky ledge that Muldoon had selected as the best line of sight for an ambush.

90

He had forbidden them to light up in case the rising tongue of smoke should prematurely alert their quarry.

The four *bandidos* had been ensconced above the entrance to the ravine for much of the day. Buzzards had zoomed by overhead to check out these biped interlopers. And various wild creatures had wandered down to the river's edge to slake their thirst. This was their first encounter with another human being.

Bull Ferris gave a sigh of relief. He was sweating like a pig in heat. It was hot as hell, and there had been no shelter from the blazing inferno that scoured the arid terrain. Being on the large side, Bull had suffered the most. He was anxious to get this business settled and head north himself.

Once he had been paid off, Ferris intended heading west to try his luck on the gold-fields of Colorado.

Muldoon took out a spyglass from his saddle-bag and aimed it towards the approaching traveller. Man and rider were still a half-mile distant.

'Sure is,' he announced with relish. Then to the others, 'Check your weapons. We don't want this dude gettin' away.'

After levering shells into the breeches of their rifles the four men settled themselves into position, and waited. Squinting eyes focused along the grey metal barrels lining up on the distant target. Index fingers nervously played with tight triggers. It was always the same when the target was of the human variety.

Bull Ferris wiped the sweat from his eyes. The minutes passed as the target drew nearer, its outline sharpening. Another hundred yards and Wallace would be within easy killing range. He settled his hat low over his eyes to block out the sun's glare. Then he rested his bewhiskered chin on the worn stock of his old 1864 Spencer.

Suddenly a deep-throated roar erupted on his left. The deafening crash bounced back off the ravine walls. It was Striker. Damn fool Kid had loosed off too soon.

But the shot had found its mark. The rider threw up his arms, tumbling out of the saddle like a rag-doll.

'You shoulda waited 'til he was nearer,' snapped Muldoon.

'I got him, didn't I?' the Kid responded with vigour.

'That don't mean he's dead,' added Ferris, rising to his feet. 'We'll have to go down and find out just how good a shot you really are.'

'Keep them guns handy,' ordered Muldoon, edging down the scattered clutch of boulders. 'He might just be playin' possum.'

Carefully the four outlaws approached the still body of Ben Wallace. It appeared as if the guy was indeed strumming with the angels.

Ferris relaxed. He made his way over to the dead man's horse. Poking out of the saddle boot was a rifle that had drawn his attention. Not the normal variety of Winchester, this was something special. He could tell by the engraved silver butt.

That was the moment when Ben Wallace chose to announce that he was still taking in oxygen. Although judging by the quantity of blood pumping from the wound, his time was fast running out. The shell had lodged in his chest barely an inch from his heart.

He groaned: a guttural snort that drew the bushwhackers up short.

'The bastard's still breathin',' yelped the Kid, stepping back as if expecting the injured man to draw on him.

'What did I tell yuh?' huffed Muldoon. 'You fired too soon.'

'This will stifle his complaining,' announced Dutch Henry stepping forward and aiming his .41 Colt Lightning at the prostrate man's head.

He was not accorded the opportunity to carry out his threat.

Another weighty boom ripped through the gorge, spinning the Dutchman on his heel. Arms waving like a windmill, a harsh gurgle issued from his yawning mouth as he crashed over on to his back. He was dead before the shot's echo had dissipated.

Before the three remaining brigands had a chance to think, two more blasts rent the air. One sent Muldoon's hat into orbit. The other chased a shiver down Kid Striker's back. He hollered loudly as the searing bite of hot lead singed his vitals.

Concealed behind the injured man's horse, Ferris had kept his cool, noting from where the puff of smoke originated: a small cluster of cottonwoods some 300 yards off the trail. He couldn't help but admire the accuracy of shooting at that range. No way could his old Spencer measure up.

But this Winchester certainly would. He whipped it out of the saddle boot, rested the long barrel against the seat and dispatched four shots in the direction of the hidden rifleman.

The gun was one of those few Winchesters that had been labelled as a 'special edition'. Very few had been made. But Bull Ferris knew about guns. He had heard rumours about these perfectly balanced firearms produced to the highest standards, but had never thought that he would ever handle one.

'Git yer asses out of here,' he hollered back to his confederates as he pumped more bullets towards the distant clump of trees, 'while I keep him pinned down.'

Muldoon signalled his understanding as he and the Kid scuttled hell for leather back towards the safety of the ravine. Ferris's shooting appeared to have the desired effect. No more angry responses emerged from their hidden assailant's lair.

Ferris backed the horse towards the Nemaha Gap, keeping his body concealed from view. With each yard gained he knew that the effectiveness of even the most accurate shootist would be diminished. Dutch Henry was left to provide dinner for the host of flies attracted by the scent of blood.

Sweating buckets. Ferris eventually made it back to his confederates unscathed.

Back in the cover of the rocks by the ravine, he abandoned the horse but kept the prized firearm. Being the proud owner of such a quality weapon would substantially raise his profile among other gunfighters.

Bull Ferris was going up in the world.

'That dude sure knows how to shoot,' he snorted, dragging a dirty bandanna across his forehead.

6

Jericho Jackson

Once the gang had scuttled back to the relative safety of Nemaha Gap, Muldoon quickly reached the conclusion that they could not hang around there for much longer. There was no way of ascertaining how many other gunnies were out there. At this very moment, a whole pack of lethal shootists could be sighting in on any stray bit of his torso that offered them an enticing target. He shivered at the thought.

Muldoon wasted no time hanging around the gorge.

'Let's get out of here,' he urged. Quickly he mounted up and swung away from the grisly scene, digging silver spurs viciously into the flanks of his cayuse. With one of his men dead and another leaking blood all over the place, this was no time for heroics.

The others quickly followed.

Having abandoned their victim's horse Bull Ferris brought up the rear. He withdrew the worn-out Spencer from its scuffed boot and tossed it into a clump of prickly-pear, replacing it with the prized Winchester.

Just ahead, it was the Kid who urgently voiced the one thing that was bugging Muldoon.

'D'yuh reckon that bluebelly will pull through, boss?'

The gang boss scowled at the notion.

'You best pray that he don't.'

'He sure looked in a bad way,' pressed Striker, anxious not to lose face.

Muldoon remained tight-lipped. They would all have to hope that Bentley Wallace was past the point of no return.

Then he allowed himself a frigid smile.

That bluebelly's Good Samaritan had been far enough away to make any possible identification of the bush-whackers impossible. So as far as Chad

Stanton was concerned, Wallace was indeed stoking up the fires of hell. And that was what he would be told on their return to Leavenworth.

But Ben Wallace was still in the land of the living, hanging on by a thread. His horse had wandered back to the scene of the shooting and was gently nuzzling her master. Just as her rough tongue dragged across his face eliciting a pained groan, a shadow fell across the injured man.

'At least you're still with us,' came a rasping voice.

Ben's saviour had remained in his place of concealment for a further ten minutes after the bushwhackers had departed. From there, he had watched intently, just in case they were lying in wait to gun him down when he showed himself. He had no way of knowing that they had feared he might in fact be a small army.

The man casually toed the supine body of Dutch Henry. Then, as an afterthought, he jabbed at the bloodied cadaver with the long barrel of a Sharps Buffalo rifle, just to confirm there was not going to be an unexpected resurrection. The Dutchman remained still. He was going nowhere, except to join up with Old Nick.

The man grunted with evident satisfaction.

He nodded at the heavy weapon.

'I can allus count on you, Old Hannah, can't I?' He grinned. It was more like a toothless cackle. 'Better'n any of them new-fangled repeaters any day.' Then, turning to the injured man, he bent down and carefully raised his head, dribbling a few drops of warm brackish water between the cracked lips.

In response, the recipient coughed violently.

'Easy there, feller,' chided the man softly. 'You just take yer time.'

Then he quickly and expertly began to cut away Ben's shirt. A brief whistle of alarm issued from the man's pursed lips when he saw the extent of the injury.

'That sure was a close call.' He sighed. 'Another half-inch and you'd have been joinin' our friend here.'

An hour later Ben's wound had been cleaned and dressed. His right arm was strapped across his chest for support. It was a further six hours before Ben at last opened his eyes. A series of tight groans warned the makeshift sawbones that his patient was coming round.

Darkness had wrapped a cloak around the sun as lengthening shadows blunted the landscape. Striations of purple mottled the western skyline. The end of another day. One that Ben Wallace was not likely to forget in a hurry. Struggling to focus his blurred vision, Ben tried to raise himself on to one elbow.

'Best not to move for a while, young feller,' his rescuer cautioned whilst easing Ben down. 'We don't want that wound opening up. Not after all the trouble I taken to cut the slug out.'

Ben shook his head in an effort to clear the fuzz from his clogged brain.

Bloodshot eyes fastened on to a tall gangly individual sitting opposite. He was sucking hard on an old brier pipe, a stone jug of moonshine in his left hand. Long grey hair straggled from beneath a coonskin cap. The rest of his gaunt features were hidden by a thick beard. A ripe odour that Ben couldn't quite place drifted across the clearing where they were camped.

But what held Ben's attention were the sharp eyes glinting in the firelight. They were of the brightest azure he had ever seen. Blue as a mountain lake in summer. Cool and piercing. And the guy couldn't be a day under sixty.

Before he could utter a word, the Good Samaritan spoke. His deep vocals were scarred by an over-indulgence of home-made hooch.

'The name's Jericho Jackson,' he said, 'I'm a buffalo-hunter.' Ben allowed himself a brief smile. So that was the smell. 'And this little beauty was ticklin' your fancy afore I dug him out.' Jackson rattled an object on a tin plate. Ben peered at the chunk of lead that had so recently been an unwelcome guest in his body. 'Lucky for you it was deflected by one of your ribs,' continued the hunter, 'else you'd have been a goner for durned sure.'

'Much obliged, Mr Jackson,' wheezed Ben.

Jackson gave his patient a quizzical regard.

'You any notion who'd want to put your lights out, Mr . . . ?'

Ben was about to fill in the missing name. He hesitated momentarily. Until he could prove his innocence, Bentley Wallace would need to disappear.

'Smith,' he said, 'Denver Smith.' He was about to add ex-United States cavalry, but stopped himself just in time. Even though this old jigger had saved his life, Ben had the good sense to realize that he would need to exercise the utmost caution until he knew who could or could not be trusted. He had his suspicions about the ambush following his untimely departure from Leavenworth.

Now was not the time to voice them.

'Must have been road agents after my poke.' Then he hurried on: 'Not that I have anything on me that'd be worth robbing.'

'So I gathered.'

Ben eyed the buffalo-hunter askance. So he had been through his belongings already. Though Ben felt he could hardly blame the old guy. You save a man, you want to know something about him.

'Do you feel like some chow?' asked Jackson, holding out a steaming plate. 'Stewed buffalo, of course.'

'Of course.' Ben grinned, accepting the proffered dish. Although extremely weak following the makeshift operation, he was still ravenous. After a few mouthfuls, his face began to assume the colour of a ripe plum. 'Never tasted buffalo-meat before,' he said.

'What d'yuh reckon then?'

'Mighty tasty . . . if a bit on the . . . spicy side.'

Jackson chuckled loudly.

'That's 'cos I like to add lots of chilli to my stews. Gives em plenty of guts.'

'You can say that again,' gasped Ben, tipping half the contents of the waterbottle down his throat.

Between mouthfuls, each of which was followed by an indulgent belch of satisfaction, the hunter elucidated his opinion of the aromatic concoction.

'Jericho Jackson's Buffalo Stew is guaranteed to have you on yer feet and dancin' a jig in no time.' He waved a spoon at the disappearing slivers of light. 'Ask anyone hereabouts. They'll tell yuh.'

Ben eyed the lethal mixture dubiously. None the less, he eventually managed to clear his plate.

'We'd best get some shut-eye,' announced Jackson, sipping at an equally thick brew of Arbuckle's coffee. 'Got to make an early start in the mornin'. We don't wanna hang around the Nemaha for too long. Just in case them varmints decide to come back and finish the job they started.'

When Ben welcomed in the new day, the sun was already clawing its way above the eastern tree-line. Shouldering aside the muted haze of the false dawn, the early warmth heralded the approach of another scorcher. Bright orange and yellow splashes replaced cooler, more subdued hues reflected off the thin cloud base.

His nostrils twitched as another aroma drew his attention. Not more buffalo!

As if reading into his thoughts, Jericho piped up. 'That's tongue you can smell.' His own angular snout wrinkled with pleasurable anticipation as he prodded at the sizzling hunk of meat. 'The Indians reckon it's the best bit. So you're privileged.'

On the far side of the campsite a strange contraption of poles had been fastened to Ben's horse.

'What's that?' he asked.

'That, my young friend, is what's

known as a *travois*,' replied Jackson. He stood up and moved across to the A-frame structure. The rear section rested on the ground behind the horse. 'My wife was a Pawnee. It was she who taught me the art.' For the briefest of seconds, a dull cast came over the old guy's leathery features. Then, like a bird in the night, it was gone as the flow resumed. 'There's no way you'll be able to ride a horse for at least a month. Not unless you figure on headin' for the happy hunting-grounds.'

On noticing Ben's uncertain regard, the old hunter smiled, 'This here travois is a lot more comfortable than you might think,' he asserted proudly. 'Especially when it's padded out with buffalo robes. Be like reclining in one of them fancy hotel beds.'

Within the hour, Ben had been secured to the travois.

After breaking camp, Jackson mounted his own cayuse which was likewise hauling a travois piled high with raw pelts. Soon they were heading east towards the Missouri and the loosely wooded hill country beyond where Jericho Jackson had his cabin.

The journey took twice as long as normal because of the slower pace necessitated by Ben's severely weakened state. So it was early evening before they reached their destination.

The cabin was single-storey and made of logs, with a stone chimney at one end. Ben could see that the door was of sawn plank below a roof cloaked with grass sod. Wooden shutters with tiny spy-holes covered the windows. Jericho Jackson was clearly a cautious man.

Another pair of horses were grazing contentedly in a corral. Whinnies of excitement echoed across the flat tableland as soon as they recognized their stable-mates.

Staked out and drying in the sun beside the cabin was a heap of dark-brown buffalo robes. And Ben counted at least fifty elongated tongues hanging from racks.

'I smoke 'em first,' averred Jackson, noting Ben's interest, 'then pack 'em up to Omaha. Got me an agent up there. Them suckers fetch big bucks in Chicago.'

'I'm headed for Council Bluffs,' said Ben. 'Hope to get fixed up as a scout for one of the wagon trains.'

'Not for a spell you ain't,' warned Jackson as he dismounted and checked on his catch. 'You can keep me company here until you're fit enough to help tote these beauties up the trail. Earn yourself a few bucks in the process.'

That first night the fever set in with a vengeance. Jackson was not surprised. He had been expecting an adverse reaction from such a critical injury. Ben's temperature shot up. Jackson knew that the next few days would be the critical period. His patient would either come through it and recover, or else . . .

Again that dark cast clouded the otherwise jovial features as he remembered.

For three days, Ben tossed and turned, his life hanging in the balance. Often he would cry out in his sleep, a meaningless jumble that Jericho couldn't figure out. One thing was for sure. With words such as disgrace, set-up and murder punched out with such acidic ferocity, the guy had a past that was no less colourful than his own.

On the fourth day the fever abated. The shivers retreated and the injured man was able to rest undisturbed by his nightmares.

Around noon he woke up at last. His chest was aching where the bullet had chewed up his insides. But apart from that he felt fine. A man was dabbing his brow with a damp cloth.

'Glad to see you made it,' said a gruff voice.

'Where am I?'

'You're in the cabin of Jericho Jackson, buffalo hunter and supplier of choice delicacies to the well-heeled.'

Ben sat up. Then offered an expressive nod. Now he recalled.

The ambush, the old guy who had saved him, the buffalo-stew, and the travois.

'How long have I been out?' he asked, gratefully accepting the hot mug of coffee.

'Nigh on five days, give or take.'

Ben whistled.

'That long. Did I nearly — '

'On the edge, mister,' Jackson interrupted with a wry grin. 'On the edge. Only my expert nursin' got you through. That and a few herbal remedies I have for such occasions.'

'Modest old cuss, ain't you?'

'Best way for a man to be when he lives alone.'

'You seem to be a man of many parts, Jericho,' smiled a grateful Ben Wallace. 'Do all of them still work?'

'You better believe it, young feller.'

Over supper that night, Ben quizzed his benefactor about his unusual name.

The old man considered thoughtfully, lighting up the brier before answering. The bowl glowed a dull red, offsetting the twinkle in his blue eyes.

'You recall the Bible story about Joshua and how he conquered the city of Jericho,' he began, puffing a cloud of smoke into the air. It was a statement of fact rather than a question.

Everybody who'd attended Sunday School knew the story. It was every kid's favourite.

The marching of priests carrying the ark of the covenant; soldiers strutting around the city; the blowing of trumpets. Then on the seventh day, the almighty holler that brought the walls of this impregnable fortress tumbling down. A song had even been written about this classic event.

'Well, it was that story that made folks call me Jericho instead of my Christian name which is Abraham.' The hunter smiled at Ben's puzzled expression. 'I didn't exactly cause a city's wall to break up. But my tale ain't that different.'

Jackson had become trusted friends of the Pawnee Indians after he had saved the chief's life with one of his elixirs. Even though he was a buffalo-hunter, and the detested enemy of the Plains Indians, Jackson's selfless action had ensured that the tribe would be forever in his debt.

Or at least, while Lone Dog still lived.

They even regarded him as some-thing of a holy man, a spiritual benefactor, and as such had accorded him almost godlike status. It certainly had its advantages.

But in some ways, the label of invincibility proved to be more of a burden than he could ever have imagined. The tribe reckoned he was a living deity, able to achieve anything, solve any problem. For such a being, nothing was impossible.

A crisis arose when he was informed that the chief's only daughter, Whisper-ing Breeze, had been captured by the Cheyenne, who were the avowed enemies of the Pawnee. They were threatening her life if the tribe did not surrender certain tribal lands that the Cheyenne reckoned were theirs by right. Direct action in the form of a frontal assault was unthinkable. Whispering Breeze would be killed instantly.

Only Buffalo Man Jackson could save her.

For days, the hunter tried to extricate himself from the predicament. But to no avail. He was the only one who could bring the young Pawnee captive safely back to the bosom of her family.

He had been reading the Bible in a vain effort to somehow gain the Almighty's help and guidance. It was the passage from the Book of Joshua that eventually gave him the idea of how to save Whispering Breeze.

'Maybe it was divine intervention,' he commented, offering a jug of moonshine to his guest. 'Or just my lucky day.'

Jackson had gathered together a dozen of the most compliant Pawnee braves and given them each a large tin plate and a ladle. Then he had them dress up in a white sheet decorated with shiny emblems from the spirit world.

The Cheyenne camp was laid out in a clearing beside a river. It was surrounded on the other three sides by loose tree-cover. Positioning the braves at set intervals around the camp but concealed within the woods, Jackson then waited for the sun to dip over the western horizon. He figured that the shadows of approaching dusk would provide an ethereal quality that would make the coming action all the more effective.

Following three owl-hoots, the braves were to bang the ladles on the plates as hard and loudly as possible whilst emerging slowly from the trees. Simultaneously, they were to utter ghostly moans.

The bizarre scheme worked perfectly. This was nothing that the Cheyenne had ever previously experienced. And they were scared rigid. The sight and sound of these unworldly spectres emerging from the trees put the fear of

Manitou into them, precipitating instant flight. Within minutes the camp had emptied. And Jackson was able to rescue the captive princess and return her to the Pawnee camp unharmed.

As a reward, Chief Lone Dog offered his daughter to the buffalo-hunter in marriage. Whispering Breeze was far more comely than many of the other Indian women he had encountered, so Jackson was more than pleased to accept. Not that he could have refused. That would have been an insult.

Nevertheless, Abraham Jackson made a point of quitting the territory in double-quick time following the wedding ceremony. He had no intention of being called upon again in a hurry to perform the impossible. Next time he might not be so fortunate. Miracles rarely come in twos.

That had been ten years ago. And the name of Jericho had quickly become a fixture that Abraham Jackson was proud to adopt.

'What happened to Whispering Breeze?'

asked Ben, his mouth still hanging wide like a stranded trout's. As with many others before him, Ben had been totally enthralled by the story.

Jackson's ebullient manner instantly faded. His ruddy face assumed a grey pallor.

Ben realized he had ventured into painful territory.

'You don't have to tell me.'

The old hunter shook his bowed head.

'She died of the cholera.' He held Ben with a bleak stare. The words caught in his throat. 'If'n you catch that, mister, there ain't nothin' I nor anybody else can do for you.' He jabbed a thumb over his shoulder. 'Buried her out back overlookin' the hills. She allus loved that view. We used to sit together of an evenin' just watchin' the sun go down.' Tears traced a narrow path down the weathered furrows of his leathery visage.

Ben remained silent. There was nothing more to be said.

7

Omaha

A month to the day after Ben had been ambushed he felt sufficiently recovered to hit the trail.

'You still want some help getting your goods to market?' he enquired of his grizzled host after informing him of his decision to leave. He was much beholden to the old hunter, without whose timely intervention he would most assuredly have been buzzard-bait.

'How else d'yuh figure on payin' for all this here expert doctorin' you've received?' Jackson snorted, tugging on a hunk of chewing baccy. Ben refused the offer to join him. It was not a habit he wished to cultivate. 'We'll kick out at first light,' added Jackson, aiming a mouthful of brown juice at a watching lizard.

The unexpected dousing saw the tiny creature scuttling away in panic. Jackson emitted a gruff chortle, then levered himself out of his favourite rocking-chair on the veranda and set about the task of sorting the various items for trade.

During the rest of that day Ben helped to load the buffalo-pelts and dried tongues on to a pair of pack-travoises.

* * *

The journey to Omaha posed no problems. It was merely a case of accompanying the east bank of the Missouri upstream in a general northerly direction. The burgeoning rail depot lay on the opposite side of the river from the staging-post of Council Bluffs. Recent emigrants from the Eastern cities had begun to favour it as a stepping-off point for Oregon, Council Bluffs being much closer to the established trail along the Platte River.

When the two men arrived in the early afternoon of the fifth day, the settlement was a hive of activity. Teams of horses with their attendant wagons lined the makeshift single street. Piles of freight littered the sidewalks waiting to be loaded. Ben couldn't help noticing that there were no families amongst the assemblage. These were all freight wagons.

Still, he should experience no difficulty here in finding work, if only as a driver. But first there was the task of trading in Jericho Jackson's buffalo catch. The old-timer had given an assurance that he would grubstake Ben from the expected pay-out.

'Omaha is on the far side of the river,' Jackson said, jabbing a gloved finger towards the far larger settlement over on the west bank. 'My agent has an office at the end of the main street.'

He nudged his mount forward, picking a way between the untidy huddle of wagons. Where once a ferry had provided passage across the surging torrent, a wooden bridge now stood.

A man stepped out of an adjacent hut and held up a hand, motioning them to rein up. He was on the short side with a bald head that glistened in the harsh sun like a new-laid egg.

'That'll be a dollar for you, and a dollar for each of your mounts,' announced the man in a flat tone that expected violent protestation at the toll-charge.

He wasn't to be disappointed.

'Four bucks!'

'Nice to see a customer that can add up for a change.' The sarcastic nuance made Jackson bristle indignantly.

'You're chargin' us for usin' a bridge?' exclaimed the wide-eyed buffalo-hunter.

'Pay up or turn around,' came back the toll-collector's terse reply, his hand extended palm upwards.

'That's daylight robbery,' spat Jackson. 'It was only two bits to use the ferry last time I came this way.'

'That was then. This is now. And it's been the going rate since the ferry was retired.' The toll-collector's voice had taken on a frosty tone. His other hand rested meaningfully on the revolver at his hip. 'If you have a complaint, take it up with the local badge-toter.' The toll-collector brusquely wagged his paw over to a building on the far side of the bridge. 'That's his office yonder.'

The two riders cast angry peepers in the direction indicated.

And there it was. A large sign affixed to a stone block-house announced that travellers were now entering the state of Nebraska and the jurisdiction of Nathan Barley — County Sheriff. Not only that, but the said lawdog was standing on the boardwalk outside his premises, a menacing rifle cradled across his chest.

'Hurry it up, mister,' snapped the toll-collector. 'You're causing a traffic jam.'

Jackson huffed and bridled at what he considered was legalized theft. But in the end, he paid the fee. There was no other choice.

'What about when we wants to come back across the river?' he asked, snatching the proffered toll-charge tickets.

The man clicked his tongue in mock exasperation.

'If you bother to read the ticket, you'll see that it says Return!' The man offered them an uproarious laugh. 'Omaha welcomes all comers . . . ' He then took a breather, the false *bonhomie* quickly vanishing to be replaced by a churlish snarl, 'even stinking buffalo-hunters.'

Ben quickly blocked Jericho's right hand, which was grabbing for the Navy Colt.

'Easy there, old-timer,' he chided. 'No sense getting off on the wrong foot now we've actually arrived.'

'That's good advice, mister.' The toll-man nodded, already eyeing his next client. Jackson deliberately nudged his horse into the portly official, knocking his bunch of toll-tickets into a nearby puddle.

'Sorry about that,' cried the buffalo-hunter stifling a derisory laugh. 'Blame the hoss. The old feller don't cotton to hustlers.'

They were across the bridge before the surprised collector could react. The altercation had not gone unnoticed by the sheriff. He gave them a hard look as they passed, whilst patting the stock of his Winchester.

'Nice friendly town you got here, Sheriff,' said Jackson twitching his moustache.

'And that's how I intend to keep it, gents,' replied the lawman. 'Enjoy your stay.'

★   ★   ★

The buyer's office was located on the far side of town near the stock-pens. Omaha had grown considerably since the railroad arrived. Many of the more permanent structures were now of brick. And numerous side-roads branched off where houses had been erected for the local residents. Like most of its kind, the central area along the main street contained its fair share of drinking parlours and other such palaces of entertainment.

Whilst Jackson headed off to locate the buyer, Ben found them both a decent hotel where he booked a couple of rooms. Then he went in search of a store dealing in used clothing. The sooner he discarded his army duds, the better. He had arranged to meet his new partner outside a saloon called the Red Feather, one of Jackson's favourite watering-holes.

It took a couple of hours of hard bargaining for Jericho Jackson to sell off his stock. But he considered himself to be an astute negotiator and at the close both parties were satisfied with the outcome, each figuring they had out-smarted the other.

The hunter strutted back up the main drag whistling a tuneless ditty. This called for a celebration. And there was no place better than the Red

Feather. He was a block west when he first noticed his partner taking a particular interest in a bedraggled paint tied up at the hitching-rail in front of the saloon.

'Some'n about that horse what's taken your fancy, Denver?' he enquired, lightly stepping down off the board-walk. 'Seems a mite flea-bitten to me.'

Ben said nothing. He continued eyeing up the animal.

'Hey, boy, you hear me?' repeated Jackson, jabbing a gnarled mitt into his partner's back. 'What's with the nag?'

Ben suddenly realized it was Jericho Jackson talking. And to him. He had completely forgotten he was using an alias.

Shrugging off the startled expression clouding his face, he quickly responded with an over-casual air. 'It's not the horse, old-timer.' He aimed a finger towards the rifle butt poking out of its scabbard. 'This here long gun belongs to me.'

'You certain of that?' asked Jackson.

'Them Winchesters are a dime a dozen out here.'

'Not this one.'

'How d'yuh figure that?'

'It was a present from my pa. A special edition. Perfect balance and action. There were only five hundred ever made. See those holes on the butt?' Jackson strained his old eyes, then nodded. 'Well that was where the brass plate was screwed on. The bastard that stole it obviously didn't want the world to see it wasn't his.'

'D'yuh know who stole it?' asked Jackson.

'Has to be one of them skunks that bushwhacked me back at Nemaha Gap.' Jackson followed the direction of his young partner's bleak gaze. 'And he must be in the Red Feather.'

'What we gonna do, then?'

'Denver' stroked his chin.

'This needs thinking on,' he murmured, backing away round the side of the saloon. A precaution, just in case the owner of the horse emerged.

Jackson provided the answer to his problem.

'How's about if'n I go inside and ask who owns the paint. Somebody's bound to pipe up.' The old guy was getting keyed up, his blue eyes animated and alive. It was just like old times back in the days of the rendezvous. 'Then I'll tell him that his cayuse has a bleeding fetlock. That should bring him hurrying outside.'

'Sounds good,' agreed Denver.

'Then it's up to you, boy.' Jackson paused eyeing his partner closely. 'Reckon you can handle it from there?'

'Don't you fret none about me, old-timer.' Denver palmed his revolver, thumbed the hammer back to half-cock and spun the cylinder. Two empty chambers. Flicking out a couple of cartridges from his shell-belt, he slid the new bullets into their slots, then released the hammer and slid the pistol back into its holster. A bleakly mirthless smile split the tanned features. 'Go to it, Jericho. And keep out of the firing-line. And make no mistake. This guy will not be walking away from this encounter. No sirree!'

Jackson sucked in a deep breath and gritted his teeth. Then he turned and disappeared round the corner into the saloon.

8

Baiting the Bull

In stark contrast to the harsh glare outside, the saloon was a blur of shadowy outlines. The sun's rays filtering through the drifting haze of tobacco-smoke were the only source of illumination.

Jackson stood awhile inside the door, allowing his eyes to accustom themselves to the saloon's gloomy interior. The place was buzzing. General chatter emanating from a myriad throats blended with the discordant hammer of a battered piano in the far corner, creating an unholy racket.

Casually, the old hunter threaded his way over to the bar, carefully assessing the patrons, trying to guess who owned the stolen rifle. He joined a line of guys hunched over their drinks at the bar that occupied the entire left side of the long, narrow room. Card-games were in progress at three tables and the roulette-wheel was in full flow.

How was he going to play this?

'What'll it be, stranger?' enquired a heavily pomaded bartender.

'Beer.'

Slurping the froth from the top of the proffered glass, Jackson considered his options. He sank the rest of the beer, then removed his pistol from its holster. Without further preamble, he pointed the barrel upwards and let fly a couple of shots. The harsh blast echoed round the smoke-filled room. Fragments of plaster detached themselves from the ceiling, fluttering down on to the heads below.

But it had the desired effect.

One minute, an ear-splitting clamour, the next total silence.

Jackson didn't wait for any untoward reaction.

'Any of you rannies own the paint tied up outside,' he shouted peremptorily, whilst holstering the revolver.

'Who wants to know?' came back an equally brusque response from a heavily bearded jasper further along the bar. The guy had his pistol cocked and poking at Jackson's head. Profound suspicion was etched on the guy's grizzled features.

Jackson didn't mince his words.

'He's gotten a bad cut on his front fetlock that needs treatin'.'

'There weren't nothin' wrong with him when I came in here,' retorted the big guy, levering himself off the bar. A deep frown scored his forehead. Hard eyes, black and flinty, bored into the old hunter.

'Well there is now,' asserted Jackson. 'Go out and see if'n you don't believe me.'

'I'll do just that,' snarled Bull Ferris, shaking the pistol in a threatening manner. 'And you better be right, feller. 'Cos if'n you ain't . . . ' The fearsome glower spoke of dire consequences coming Jackson's way should the old guy's disclosure prove groundless.

Denver had positioned himself in the middle of the street. He had been all set to blast the rifle's illicit owner as soon as he emerged from the saloon. Further consideration, however, reminded him that this would be counter-productive and would likely see him being arrested for murder.

And anyway, he needed this polecat to spill the beans as to why that bunch of backshooters had tried to kill him at Nemaha Gap. Better all round to give the rat an even break.

The two shots from inside the Red Feather rendered him tense and expectant as his gun hand hovered above the butt of his pistol.

Next thing, the doors of the saloon slammed open and a big hulk of a man emerged. He was followed by a chuntering herd of curious onlookers. Ferris stopped, screwing up his eyes against the brightness, then stepped off the boardwalk and bent down to determine the extent of the supposed injury.

Nothing.

The leg was clear. Not a speck of blood to be seen.

Puzzlement clouded Bull Ferris's ugly mush. Then he uttered a manic howl of rage. The growl erupting from deep within his bulky frame sounded like a bursting volcano. That was when Denver made his play.

'Where did you get that Winchester, asshole?' he rapped tersely.

Ferris spun on his heel to face this challenge from an unexpected quarter. His mouth dropped open.

Again Denver repeated his question.

'That rifle you're toting.' His words were delivered in a composed, even tone. 'Where did it come from?'

'Who in hell's name are you?'

The question didn't require an answer.

Bull Ferris, although not the sharpest tack in the box, was rapidly arriving at the conclusion that he had been set up. And that this guy, however unlikely it appeared, was the jigger whom he and the boys had ambushed at Nemaha Gap. Not only was the dude still alive, but he was also after avenging himself on his attackers.

'I'm the guy that wants to know how you got hold of my rifle,' persisted Denver.

Ferris just stared, nonplussed.

Then his devious mind began to function again. Beady eyes studied his adversary from beneath hooded brows. The guy was just standing there in the middle of the street, unheeding, hands loose by his side, not even near the pistol on his hip.

Then Ferris realized that he was still clutching his own sixgun, and it was already cocked. All he had to do was haul off and this poor sap would be pushing up the daisies. Easy as falling off a log.

His thick rubbery lips drew back in a mocking grin. The gun lifted, a curled finger tightening on the trigger.

Afterwards, none of the watching throng could positively assert that they had witnessed Denver Smith drawing his gun. It had happened in a single blurred movement, in the blink of an eye.

Two shots broke the tense silence on Main Street. Although only a single bullet hole was visible, both had struck their target, such was the accuracy of the shooting.

Ferris staggered back under the impact from the heavy .44 slugs. His eyes glazed over. Clutching at his stomach, he slumped to the ground, blood pouring from between his gnarled fingers.

'Is he dead?' called out a voice from the watching crowd.

'If he ain't now, it won't be long,' answered another. 'That was a gut shot.'

Denver holstered his gun and hurried across to the wounded outlaw. He had deliberately aimed low to avoid an outright killing shot.

Ferris saw him coming through rapidly dimming vision. But he still had enough strength left to raise his gun hand. The thumb clawed back the trigger.

Standing on the edge of the mob, Jericho Jackson was in a position to witness the surreptitious move. Hurling himself across the intervening space with a vigour that belied his advancing years, Jackson lunged at the prodding revolver. A second after his boot connected, the barrel spat flame. But the deadly load whistled harmlessly skyward.

'That's the second time you've saved my bacon, Jericho,' gasped Denver, sucking in a lungful of oxygen. That had been a close call. 'This is getting to be something of a habit.'

'I'll give you my bill later,' Jackson grinned.

Just then the injured man groaned. It was a potent reminder to Denver that there was much he needed to find out from the dying outlaw. With little thought for the man's well-being, he grabbed his shirt-front and shook him roughly.

'So why were you and those other skulking backshooters after gunning me down,' he railed angrily. 'What have I ever done to you?'

Ferris groaned louder.

'Come on, out with it!'

'Why should I tell you anythin'?' gasped Ferris, his words slurred and uneven.

'Because if you don't I'll finish off what I started.' Denver jabbed the snout of his pistol into the injured man's ear. 'Now talk!'

'Go piss at the moon!' croaked Ferris, his seamed face twisted in pain. 'I'm gonna peg out anyway.' He shuddered as a stabbing jolt of agony lanced through his mashed guts.

Denver leapt to his feet all set to blast the outlaw into the great beyond. It was the placatory hand of Jericho Jackson that urged him to adopt a more conciliatory approach.

Pulling Denver over to one side, he whispered. 'Why not offer to send for a doctor. Persuade him that he ain't headin' for Boot Hill just yet awhile. And that *when* he pulls through, you won't press charges if he spills the beans on his sidekicks.'

'Erm!' murmured Denver, offering his partner a wry smile. 'How come you're always so full of bright ideas, old man?'

'Us Jacksons come from privileged stock,' averred the oldster with evident pride.

'You don't mean . . . '

Jackson tapped his jutting snout knowingly.

'Enough said.'

The ruse worked.

Persuaded that he wasn't immediately bound for the devil's kitchen, Ferris opened up. He was only a hired hand, so the information he had to impart was of limited value. But it was better than nothing.

He had been working for a gambler by the name of Polkadot Charlie Muldoon but had lit out after the pay-out, intending to head West to try his luck on a newly discovered gold-strike in Colorado.

Ferris ardently professed that it wasn't he who had shot Denver, but a young gunnie who went under the handle of Kid Striker because of his red hair. The gang had been hired by an army officer to rob the Fort Leavenworth payroll. When Denver pressed him on this point, Ferris had no idea who or why. Only that somebody on the fort wanted to put the kibosh on a certain young captain.

The mystery ill-wisher was not content with hounding his victim out of the army, he wanted him dead and buried. So when the disgraced bluecoat fled the state, Muldoon was paid to follow and finish the business once and for all.

Jericho Jackson's untimely intervention at Nemaha Gap had spoiled all that. The old hunter shot his partner a confused look. This was a new revelation that Denver Smith had not seen fit to make. Jackson had wondered at the army trousers, the tell-tale Stetson minus the braided hatband, and the black holster etched with the Third Cavalry badge.

But like all frontiersmen, he balked at the notion of questioning a man's past. If he was to help in bringing his partner's attackers to justice, then maybe the time was fast approaching when questions would need to be posed, and answers given.

For the moment at least, that would have to wait.

'So where are they now?' asked Denver trying to maintain his cool. 'Have they gone back to Leavenworth?'

Ferris was rapidly fading. His creased skin was waxy and pale, eyes glassy as death stared out vacantly from the hollow sockets. Both Denver and his partner knew that the injured outlaw would not survive for much longer. So did the surrounding bystanders.

'Keep back,' ordered Jackson. 'Give the guy some air.' But he was more concerned about Ferris clamming up if he cottoned on to any terminal predictions regarding his imminent meeting with the grim reaper.

Ferris shook his head.

'Muldoon received a wire. The next day he and the Kid headed west, bound for Wyoming.' Ferris gulped, his breathing shallow and depressed. 'Where's that sawbones you promised?' The plea emerged as a choked gurgle.

'Don't worry, feller,' stressed Jackson. 'I can see him hurryin' down the street right now.'

This seemed to calm Ferris. He nodded gratefully.

'Anything else?' urged Denver.

'I know they've gotten an army contact . . . and are intendin' to pick up a cache of rifles . . . sell 'em to the Cheyenne.'

Mention of the Cheyenne found Jericho Jackson taking a more than passing interest.

'Rifles for the Cheyenne you say?'

'Muldoon reckons . . . they're after wipin' out their most . . . deadly enemy.'

'And who might that be?'

'The . . . Pawnee.'

Jackson's whole body tensed. His blue eyes shrank to pinpricks, brittle and hard as granite.

'Wyoming's a big territory. Whereabouts?' It was now the hunter who was pressing for information.

Ferris wheezed and coughed up a stream of thick red gunge.

'Come on, out with it,' urged Jackson. 'Where they headed?'

'The town of . . . Saratoga was mentioned. That's all I . . . know.'

That was the end for Bull Ferris. He keeled over and lay still.

But it was enough.

'This feller don't need a sawbones,' announced Jackson to nobody in particular. 'Somebody go fetch the undertaker.'

'What happened here?' came a guttural demand to their rear. It was the sheriff.

'This guy tried to gun down my partner when he asked for his rifle back,' replied Jackson. 'He only defended himself. The guy had stolen it and was gonna shoot him.'

'That's the truth of it, Sheriff,' agreed the bartender of the Red Feather. 'It was self-preservation. And the fastest draw I've ever seen here in Omaha.'

'Anywhere else for that matter,' remarked another onlooker. Nods and muttered comments corroborated opinions of the stranger's prowess with a handgun.

'Anyone else here prepared to back up this feller's claim that he fired in self-defence?' Sheriff Barley peered around, almost challenging the onlookers to say their piece.

Three men stuck their hands in the air. Others merely offered a curt nod. It seemed that the two strangers were in the clear. Of late, action in Omaha had been rather low-key. Nathan Barley would have enjoyed the prestige of a cut-and-dried murder trial followed by a juicy hanging. He would have to curb his impatience.

There was too much supporting evidence confirming that Bull Ferris had made the first move, thus forcing the lawman to accept Denver's innocence.

'Seems like the law's on your side, mister,' conceded the tin star somewhat grudgingly. His droopy moustache twitched. 'But we don't welcome gun-happy drifters in Omaha. So I want you out of town by noon tomorrow.'

With that, the sheriff departed to resume his vigil on the porch fronting his office.

9

Wyoming Bound

The church clock was striking the noon hour as Denver Smith and Jericho Jackson nudged their horses down the main street of Omaha. Denver had intended saying his farewells to the old hunter and heading West alone. But Jackson was adamant that he was coming along. And not just for the ride. If his old friends the Pawnee were in trouble, he wanted to lend his support to even out the score.

And if that meant going up against a gang of low-life pesky gunrunners, then that was the way it had to be.

The old hunter tugged on the lead rein of the packmule he had bought for the protracted journey across the rolling grasslands of Nebraska. After making enquiries at the office of the Overland

Stage Line, he had discovered that Saratoga was close to Fort Laramie.

'That must be where they're getting the guns from,' announced Jackson, chewing on a wad of tobacco.

'I'm wondering if the same varmint that had me cashiered is behind all this.'

That was Denver Smith's first mention of his past. It seemed to Jackson that this was as good a time as any to broach the subject.

'If'n we're gonna be partners in this jaunt,' posited the hunter in rather a diffident manner, 'maybe now's the time to get things out in the open. I done told you about my dealings with the Pawnee.' He paused, shifting his gaze across to the younger man. 'You gotten anything on your mind, Denver?'

The ex-cavalryman stared ahead. His face had a vacant look, the blank eyes focusing on the distant horizon.

Then he spoke in a low voice. His words were barely audible and Jackson had to strain to hear what was being said.

'First off,' began the young man, 'My name is not Denver Smith.' Jackson coughed to hide his surprise but remained tight-lipped. 'It's Captain Bentley Wallace. Or should I say, ex-Captain, late of the Third United States Cavalry based at Fort Leavenworth.'

His dark eyes clouded over, shrinking to brittle lumps of coal. The square jaw, set firm and unyielding, jutted forward. Venomous hatred which had been simmering in the young man's soul all these weeks past since that horrific episode came pouring out like a volcanic eruption.

'I decided to change my name so nobody would cotton to my having been cashiered. Denver was the town of my birth, and I figured that anybody with a name like Smith would be easily forgotten.' He hurried on, now anxious to reveal all to his new friend and confidant. 'I didn't say anything because I figured we would be parting company after selling your goods in Omaha. And the fewer jaspers who knew my true identity the better.'

Ben went on to relate all that had happened since that nightmarish scenario had unfolded back on the evening of the payroll robbery.

It was early evening before he had fully unburdened his soul. Lengthening shadows of the approaching sunset reminded both men that they had not eaten since early morning.

*　*　*

After leaving Omaha behind, they had headed due west. For the first couple of days they rode steadily, passing numerous recently settled farmsteads dotted about as ever more immigrants from the East set down roots. After leaving the last farm behind, Ben quickly came to appreciate that they were truly on the edge of the known civilization.

As they ploughed through an ocean of grassland that brushed the undersides of their mounts there were few landmarks to act as guide. Except along the creek banks, trees were always in short supply. And with the constant Plains wind in their faces, it was like swimming against the tide. Only by heading directly into the setting sun could they be certain of their direction.

'This is as good a place as any to make camp,' averred Jackson, drawing his cayuse to a halt in a shallow draw beside a narrow creek. He unhooked a red bandanna from around his neck and wiped the sweat from his furrowed brow. 'Once we hit the Platte, it'll be easier.'

Ben stepped down out of the saddle and stretched his tired muscles.

'I was hoping to get a job as a scout once I reached Omaha,' said Ben, lighting up a stogie. 'Head west, then make a new start in the territories. But now all I want to do is find this skunk Polkadot Muldoon and squeeze the truth out of the rat's scurvy guts. Find out who really did the dirty on me.'

Jackson's eyes followed his partner's retreating back as he wandered away, head bowed and deep in thought. The old-timer shook his head as he unloaded the mule. Revenge can eat away at a man's soul, his very being, until there ain't nothing left worth the saving. He could only pray that Ben Wallace would find his own salvation before it was too late.

★   ★   ★

Two days later, as they were edging down a gully that funnelled into a shallow creek bottom, Ben noticed a dark cloud on the horizon. At first he took it for a rain cloud and the approach of a storm.

'Best get our slickers on,' he suggested to the dozing figure by his side as he reached behind the cantle to unhook the yellow tarp.

'Uh?' mumbled Jericho, whose attention had been lulled into a comatose state of lethargy by the drab Nebraska landscape.

Ben pointed to the dark mass that

even now was blotting out the sun. Not only that, but it was moving at a rapid pace and would be on them soon. Funny thing was, thought the younger man, squinting at the ominous blot, it appeared to be shimmering, emitting an iridescent sparkle.

He gave a nervous grunt, half-laugh, half-cough. It could almost be alive, such was the bubbling ferment that appeared to be pulsating from deep within its very core.

Maybe it was in the nature of the Plains to throw up these strange cloud formations.

Both men had reined in their mounts, staring at the rapidly closing singularity. It was Jackson who broke the uneasy silence. He laid a gnarled hand over his eyes to filter out the sun's glare before voicing his reaction. The comment that emerged was both biting and cogent, laced with a mixture of fear and respect.

'That ain't no storm cloud, mister.'

'What else could it be, then?'

'A damn blasted plague of hoppers, that's what.' His blue eyes widened as the horror of the approaching vision from hell drew ever closer. Now little more than a half-mile distant, they could just make out the insistent drone from millions of gossamer wings hammering at the air. 'Another two minutes and they'll be on us.'

Jackson hurriedly dismounted, dragging his mount to the ground behind a cluster of rocks. Frantically waving his arms, he indicated for a stunned Ben Wallace to follow suit.

The swarm was over a mile wide and acting like a total eclipse of the sun. It was as if darkness had fallen six hours early. Already the first insects were settling on to the exposed skin of their faces, checking out their suitability as a source of food. Ben shook himself, batting off the loathsome creatures.

'Are they fatal to humans?' he enquired nervously in a tremulous tone. This was his first experience of a grasshopper invasion.

'Only if you get smothered under their weight,' responded Jackson, wrapping himself in his slicker. He was forced to raise his voice above the increasing barrage of sound. It emerged as a guttural rasp. 'And that ain't as crazy as it sounds. Just dig in and hope they pass us by. There ain't nothin' else around here worth stoppin' for that I can see.'

Ben pulled his hat low over his pinched face and followed the buffalo-hunter's lead.

Within a minute, the deafening onslaught slammed into them. It felt as if they were being pelted by hailstones and Ben was more than glad of the protection offered by the heavy rain-slicker.

The frightened horses had to be constantly reassured with gentle pats and measured words to prevent them from panicking. Surrounded by the screaming wail, like an angry banshee, it was no mean task even for an ex-cavalryman.

The passage of the hopper swarm lasted for ten minutes, although to Ben it seemed like an hour. At last a silence that was almost palpable settled over the grim scenario.

Squirming out from beneath their temporary shelter, the two partners shrugged off the thick layer of insects that covered everything in sight. Most departed with a churlish buzz. But not all. Vigorously, they slapped at their bodies to get rid of the hateful creatures.

It was, however, still necessary to strip down to their underclothes to ensure that none remained. And like monkeys in a zoo, the two travellers had to poke and probe each other's nether regions before they were satisfied that the last insect had eventually been dispatched to join its deceased comrades.

It was agreed that a pot of strong coffee and a couple of cigars were needed to calm jangled nerves after such a nail-biting ordeal. Ben's nails that was. Jericho had seen it all before.

'Them critters can wipe out an entire farmer and his stock,' he mused, sipping the thick brew. Grimacing, he laced it with a generous measure from the moonshine jug which he then handed to Ben before continuing. 'I've seen 'em munch their way through a whole field of corn in fifteen minutes, then devour the leaves and bark off every tree in sight.' He shook his head sadly. 'Not a pretty sight, I can tell yuh. They'd have even stripped the clothes off our backs if'n we hadn't taken cover. Yes sirree,' the old-timer expounded, puffing out a head of blue smoke, 'I've known many a sodbuster that's had to give up and head back East following a visit from the hoppers.'

'Think we'll meet up with another bunch?' asked an impressed Ben Wallace.

Jackson afforded the grave query a casual shrug of indifference.

'In the lap of the gods, son. Just like most things that happen out here.'

Two hours after being hit by the strange *rain cloud*, the travellers had crossed the dry wash of the Little Blue and were heading into the lowering sun.

As if to confirm Jericho Jackson's astute observations regarding the back-breaking toil of making it as a dirt farmer, they came upon the decaying remnants of an old soddy. Abandoned to the ravages of the sun-baked prairie, the wizened husk testified to the ease with which nature can so quickly reclaim her own. The bleached remnants of this once thriving homestead confirmed that only the stubbornly resilient would survive the harsh environment.

And there, nailed to the rotting doorpost in faded green was the previous owner's opinion of his new found piece of *El Dorado*. Barely discernible, the peeling message had been issued as a warning to others who sought to tame the wilderness. It read: *Busted by grasshoppers that left nothing but the mortgage.*

'There ain't no answer to that,' murmured Jackson, spearing the notice with a jaundiced eye. 'It's one reason I never set down permanent roots. Back-breaking toil from dawn 'til dusk with the devil on your back every step of the way.'

A cold shiver chased the demons of death down Ben's spine. He could not help but ponder that man's hold on to life in this grimly austere corner of the frontier was both perilous and temporary, so easily snuffed out in the blink of an eye.

The lonely outpost was thankfully soon left behind.

⋆　⋆　⋆

It was another four days before they hit the Platte, a squirming stretch of water having its origins many hundreds of miles to the west in the sprawling fastness of the Rocky Mountains. The twin tracks carved out along the north bank by an endless procession of

West-bound wagons were visible for miles.

Ben had expected to see a procession of the white-topped Conestogas making their way steadily westwards. He was a little disappointed when the view in all directions proved to be empty, devoid of all human contact.

Jackson picked up on his partner's disquiet. He stepped down from the saddle and studied the churned-up ground.

'This trail is at least a month old,' he observed, prodding at a thick cowpat. 'The last train to have passed through here will be up around South Pass by now.'

'I was hoping we could have joined up with one for a spell,' muttered Ben rather disconsolately. 'Give me a chance to get in some scouting practice.'

'We're near into August now,' remarked Jackson. 'Wagon trains that hope to reach Oregon before the winter snows set in will have had to have left Council Bluffs by the middle of May.

And believe me when I tell yuh, boy, that nobody in their right mind would want to get stuck in the mountains over winter.'

After letting their mounts slake their thirst, the two riders remounted and resumed their trek.

10

Paradise Villa

Four weeks to the day after packing out of Omaha, Bentley Wallace and Jericho Jackson crossed into Wyoming territory. They had left the comforting familiarity of the Oregon Trail at Scottsbluff, striking south-west across the broken country of the Medicine Bow range. Surging ranks of dark pine had taken over from the endless waves of rolling grassland.

It was a welcome change of scenery, but the increasingly steep and winding trails slowed onward progress to that of a recalcitrant tortoise. Cresting a mountain pass known as the Chugalug, Jackson hauled rein and checked his ancient timepiece. Its melodically dulcet chimes echoed between the austere bands of grey rock that lined the narrow causeway.

The minute-hand having come loose, he reckoned it was close to the noon hour.

He peered down into the valley below. A broad amphitheatre shrouded in muted tones of brown, grey and gilded orange stared back. Acres of dry grassland were interspersed with stands of cottonwood. Flanked by blunt ridges sporting knotty capstones, the whole feature was enclosed within towering bluffs of red sandstone.

And in the middle of this natural Arcadia sat a huddle of ugly black buildings. A trading-post that laughing referred to itself as Paradise Villa. The owner clearly had a sense of humour. Approaching this unlikely oasis, they couldn't help noticing that it even had a palm tree to enhance the exotic appeal. Although closer inspection revealed it to be a wooden effigy badly in need of repainting.

'Could be we can find out if Muldoon and his bunch passed through here recently,' remarked Jackson, instinctively checking the load of his Sharps. Casually he rested it across his lap before gingerly nudging his mount down the narrowly twisting trail of loose stones. Ben followed behind.

When they arrived some forty minutes later, there were another four horses at the hitch rail, each with a bedroll tied behind, indicating that travellers, like themselves, were just passing through.

Shouldering through the doorway, Ben quickly narrowed his gaze to acclimatize to the shadowy haze inside. First impressions confirmed that Paradise was a somewhat optimistic way to describe the place. Although at least the owner had made some efforts to embellish his premises. Various skins ranging from beaver to cowhide covered the walls and were supplemented by Indian blankets and beadwork.

Jackson immediately recognized the work of the Pawnee, which was well represented.

His shifty eyes quickly scanned the furthermost recesses of the room. It always paid to be observant. A man's life could depend on knowing from where a potential danger might threaten. The owners of the four horses outside were sat round a table over by the window, except there were only three of them.

Maybe the fourth was at the privy.

Directly in front was the bar, a long piece of roughly sawn timber supported by two large barrels.

'What'll it be, strangers?' bellowed a large bluff individual, whose thickly knotted arms were vigorously endeavouring to scrub a hole in the bar-top. A black beard tinged with grey hovered above a bulging girth revealing teeth stained yellow by too much baccy chewing. 'Only the finest beer is served at Paradise Villa. Fresh in only yesterday from the brewery in Laramie. Or maybe your penchant is for the best rye whiskey this side of Purgatory.' His large belly shook with glee. 'And we got some real tasty victuals on offer today.'

'Two beers and some information is all,' replied Jackson, holding the proprietor's unctuous leer.

The two newcomers accepted their drinks and sunk the jugs in a single draught. At least the guy was right. It was indeed good ale. Jackson wiped the foam from his white-flecked whiskers and pushed his glass across for a refill.

'Told yuh, didn't I? Only the finest beer in the territory is served at Panhandle Pete Carver's place.'

'Now about that information,' continued Jackson evenly.

Before the proprietor could reply, a young Indian girl came through from the kitchen at the rear of the premises to clear away the empty platters on the table. She was no more than eighteen years old. And from the decorations adorning her buckskin shift, Jackson could immediately see that she was of the Pawnee tribe. Maybe she was even from his old camp.

His interest was immediately aroused. He quickly noted that she was no ordinary squaw, the elaborate patterns embroidered on her buckskin over-shirt pointing to a high-born lineage.

After gathering the plates together, she was about to leave when one of the men, a heavy jasper with straggly red hair, grabbed her round the waist and lifted her unceremoniously on to his knee.

'Not so fast there, girl,' he hawked as the Indian woman struggled to escape. 'How about a little dessert? I'm still a mite peckish, and it ain't for no apple-pie, neither.'

His sidekicks perked up, anticipating their own participation in the forthcoming entertainment.

'Red's gotten hisself a peckish pecker,' chuckled a thin weasel to his companion. 'What do you say to that, Montana?'

'Sure beats rat-stew,' scoffed the third man.

Red slid his hand under the girl's skirt. She cried out, pummelling at his burly frame. But her efforts were puny and ineffectual.

'Quit your squirmin', girl.' The brittle command was accompanied by a stiff backhander. It drew blood from the girl's split lip.

Jackson had seen more than enough. He raked back the hammer of the Sharps. The double click of the ratchet bounced off the wooden walls. But it had the desired effect. No man could mistake that sound.

The man called Red stiffened.

'Just let her go and apologize for the inconvenience caused,' said the old hunter, pointing the long barrel at the bulging torso of the hardcase. 'Then we'll say no more about it.' The order emerged as a scathing hiss.

'And if'n I don't?' Red's reply was blunt and challenging.

'Then I'll spread your ugly carcass all over that back wall.' Jackson drew the Sharps into his shoulder, sighting down the barrel. 'And make no mistake, feller. At this range, I cain't hardly miss.

You ever seen what a Sharps 'Big Fifty' can do to a man?' He shook his head expressively. 'Not a pretty sight.'

But Red knew that the old guy wouldn't haul off whilst he was holding on to the woman. His lips drew back in a mirthless grin. The jigger was bluffing. His hand slid down to the holstered revolver concealed on his blind side.

'You some kinda squaw-lover, mister?'

'Nope!' replied Jackson. 'Just a feller that hates bad-mannered skunks like you.'

Red scowled but didn't appear in any rush to release the girl.

Ben had shifted his position to cover the other two men, both staring goggle-eyed at the threatening buffalo-gun.

The girl sensed her captor's sly movement. His arm was still tightly gripping her round the waist. But she knew where his intentions lay. It was now up to her to thwart his crafty scheme. Red's beady eyes were levelled at the old man holding the rifle.

Twisting her head, she lunged open-mouthed at his exposed left ear, and bit down hard.

A scream of agony erupted from the bullish toad's throat. He released the girl and lifted his hand to the damaged appendage. At the same time, the girl took advantage of the distraction to dart behind the bar, where she spat out her bloodied trophy.

But Red was no pushover. A saloon brawler, used to all manner of trickery, he uttered an irate howl, then hurled himself to one side whilst palming his own gun. He figured to catch the old-timer off guard.

He was wrong.

A heavy blast shook the very foundations of the wooden structure. In the enclosed space, it sounded like the salvo from an army field battery. A dark hole, ragged and big as a man's fist, appeared in the middle of Red's chest as the impact of the lethal shell slammed him back against the wall.

Before the echo had died away

Jackson had slid a new round into the breech and swung the large gun to cover the other two.

Four hands touched the rough ceiling, such was their desire to avoid a similar fate to their leader's.

'Ease off there mister,' crowed the sweating weasel. 'We don't want no trouble. Red always did try to push his luck.'

'All he'll be pushing up soon are the daisies,' commented Jackson acidly. 'Now get that piece of trash outa here.' The buffalo-hunter turned away to finish his drink as the two cowed range bums complied. 'Now about that information,' he continued, coolly addressing the gaping maw of Panhandle Pete as if nothing untoward had occurred.

Ben was about to join him when he notice the shadow of a newcomer suddenly appear on the floor where the sun's rays were beaming in through the open door.

The fourth man!

They had forgotten all about him.

And Jericho had his back to the guy. Luckily, the elusive man had not seen Ben, who was concealed behind the door. There was no time to lose. Quick as a flash, he raised his boot and rammed it against the door. A croak of pain informed Ben that his aim had been true. The shadow disappeared along with its owner.

He grabbed open the door, drew his revolver and stepped outside. Scrabbling about in the dust was a Mexican, still wearing his sombrero and a lurid snarl beneath the drooping moustache. His searching hand found the fallen gun. He rolled to one side as he sought to catch his adversary off guard. Ben's first shot ploughed up a plume of sand where the man had been seconds before.

The Mex's own weapon spat lead and flame, missing Ben's head by a cat's whisker. Slivers of wood from the door-jamb peppered his face. But they were not enough to sour Ben's aim. But just to make certain, he emptied the rest of the chamber into the stubborn Mexican. Only with the last slug chewing a hole in his tough hide did the ornery greaser deign to call it a day.

White smoke drifted across the grim scene of death. Paradise Villa was not having one of its more enchanting days.

Back inside the cabin, Jackson handed Ben his drink which the younger man sank gratefully. Eyes agog, it took him some minutes to recover his composure.

'Perhaps we can get to that information now,' the buffalo man demanded vehemently.

'Anything you want to know, gents,' spluttered Panhandle Pete, anxious to prevent any further bloodletting, particularly where he was concerned. 'Just ask away and I'll do my best to accommodate you.'

'First off,' began Jackson, aiming his query at the cowering Indian girl, 'What's a Pawnee princess doing servin' on tables in a dump like this?'

'Princess?' scowled Carver derisively.

'I bought her fair and square off'n a couple of Cheyenne braves who passed this way.'

'When was that?'

'Must be about a month back.' Pete gave the question a puzzled frown. He had no love for redskins. They were there to be used and discarded. And he was baffled that another white man didn't feel the same. But clearly, this guy had something going with the Pawnee. 'I gave them some firewater and a couple of old Springfields to keep 'em happy. Anythin' wrong with that, mister?'

Jackson made no attempt to conceal his disgust. Then he reached into the pocket of his buckskin jacket.

'Well, I'll give you ten golden eagles for her,' said Jackson, tossing a pile of coins on to the bar top. 'She's comin' with us.'

Carver shrugged. They could have her with pleasure for that much dough.

'Now about that information,' continued Jackson. 'Have a couple of guys passed this way in recent weeks? One's a fancy dude wearing a spotted vest and grey derby. The other is a mean-eyed kid with flaming red hair.'

Pete made as if to consider the question, rolling his eyes and shaking his head. He was always loath to hand out information about previous clients. You never could tell when they might turn up like bad pennies and exact revenge.

'Nobody answering to that description has called here,' he stressed, pouring himself a glass of whiskey. But the thin film of sweat beading his brow told a different tale.

'You certain of that,' pressed Ben, arrowing the guy with a penetrating glower.

'Sure I'm sure.' Pete's persuasive bluster was convincing. It was a charade he had perfected over the years. 'The guys you're after ain't passed through here.'

'He lies!'

The terse contradiction came from

over in the corner where the Pawnee girl had been watching. This was the first time that a white eyes had shown concern for her. Most of the drifters who called at the trading post were roughnecks intent only on satisfying their own depraved needs. These two were different.

The old one looked vaguely familiar. Somewhere in the depths of her memory, Swooping Owl felt she had come across him before.

Again the blunt accusation cut through the taut atmosphere like a knife through butter. Dark mahogany eyes blazed with a fierce intensity, burning deep into the back of her detested custodian.

'The pig lies! The men you describe came through here two weeks past.'

'Shut your mouth, squaw,' snarled Panhandle Pete. His fists clenched tight, the pockmarked visage creasing in panicky anger as a bright flush coloured his hollow cheeks. Turning back to the two travellers, he said, 'Don't listen to her. She don't know nothin'.'

'Polkadot Charlie Muldoon and Kid Striker are the men you seek.'

The statement was delivered in a flat monotone which made its impact all the more plausible. Swooping Owl's scornful gaze challenged the Paradise Villa proprietor to deny the truth of her assertion.

The die was cast. For Panhandle Pete Carver there was only one course of action left. His hand snaked below the counter and surreptitiously enfolded the ivory grip of the Colt Lightning he retained for just such an eventuality as this. Beady eyes, cold as a mountain stream, surveyed the two men facing him.

Both had holstered their revolvers and the Sharps was laid across a table out of reach. The small gun rose above the level of the counter, the trigger-finger blanched white as it tightened. Even a mean shootist of Ben Wallace's calibre was no match for a gun jabbing at his stomach.

Time stood still as Carver's oily grin washed over them.

Was this the end of their quest?

Then the greasy smirk changed to a guttural croak. The red face turned ashen. A thin trickle of red seeped from between Pete's tightly-clenched teeth as the revolver slipped from nerveless fingers. Staggering back, Pete Carver twisted on his heel, crashing into a line of bottles on the rear shelf. He was dead before his body hit the dirt floor.

And there, stuck between his shoulder blades — one of the knives normally used as an eating utensil.

Swooping Owl casually strolled across and hawked a mouthful of spittle at the prone cadaver. She dug into the pocket of her deceased keeper and extracted the ten dollar coins and handed them to Jackson.

'Swooping Owl not for sale,' she stated firmly.

Jackson's eyebrows raised in stunned surprise on hearing the name.

'You ain't by any chance the second daughter of Lone Dog, are you?' he questioned.

'You know my father?'

'We go back aways,' answered Jackson. His eyes misted over. 'I married your elder sister, Whispering Breeze.'

'Buffalo Man Jackson!' The tight exclamation was uttered with an equal measure of surprise.

'I recall when you were knee-high to a grasshopper,' continued Jackson, shaking his head in wonder. 'You sure have grown some.' He couldn't help noticing the admiring looks emanating from his partner. Swooping Owl certainly was one comely gal. 'How is old Lone Dog these days?'

'Father in good health, but still worried about Cheyenne taking over our hunting-lands. There have been many fights since you left with Whispering Breeze. I was captured during one of their more recent raids.'

'Some things never seem to change,' muttered Jackson. At the mention of his wife, the old hunter's face had assumed the pained grimace of a man who had been through the mill.

The Indian girl quickly latched on to his anguish.

'Where is Whispering Breeze?' she enquired cautiously.

Jackson's silence said it all.

It was Ben who put his partner's grief into words. 'She died of the cholera.'

Swooping Owl's expression remained bland, unmoving.

'It is the way,' she murmured, a comforting hand resting on the old guy's arm.

But this was not the time for past troubles to absorb their thoughts. Ben brought the conversation back to their current situation.

'If the Cheyenne get hold of any repeating rifles,' he said pointedly, 'your people won't stand a hope in hell.'

'And these guys we're following,' cut in Jackson firmly, decisively shrugging off the lethargic torpor that, for a moment, had threatened to engulf him, 'that's just what they're intendin' to do. Sell guns to the Cheyenne.'

'I remember the young one called Striker. He mention they were heading for Saratoga,' remarked the girl.

Ben nudged his partner. 'Backs up what Bull Ferris told us.'

Jackson acknowledged the remark with a poignant nod.

'And if they're two weeks in front, there ain't no time to lose,' he said, gathering up the Sharps and making to leaving the trading post. 'We can take you back to your people on the way,' he said to the Indian girl. 'Won't be much of a detour over the Elk Horn range to Rawhide Creek.'

'But first I make you good meal,' insisted Swooping Owl. She retired to the kitchen area where she busied herself with the preparations. 'Make better time with full stomach, yes?'

There was no argument there.

By mid-afternoon, with the horses watered and grained, and their supplies replenished, they were once again on the trail, this time accompanied by the alluring presence of Swooping Owl. And in that respect, Ben Wallace certainly wasn't complaining.

11

Saratoga

'How much longer have we gotta stay in this flea-pit?'

Kid Striker operated on a short fuse at the best of times. His outburst was the result of being cooped up in the old abandoned miners' cabin for upwards of a week. Sure, they had enough grub, and were well stocked up with dime novels to while away the hours. But Muldoon had banned hard liquor. He knew the effect of rot-gut whiskey on young guns such as Kid Striker. It made them tetchy and bad-tempered, liable to sound off at the slightest thing.

Muldoon scowled at his young sidekick.

The other two rannies whom he had picked up in Fort Laramie eyed the petulant young gunslinger uneasily. They had seen his caustic temper in action soon after leaving the army post when he had taken umbrage over a Pawnee woman who had refused his fumbling attempts at seduction.

That had been in a squalid trading post laughingly named Paradise Villa. When the girl had slapped his face, the others had treated it as a joke. But Striker didn't see the funny side. He had been all for carving up the Indian serving-girl with his Bowie knife. Only the swift and decisive intervention of Polkadot Muldoon had prevented blood being spilt.

The kid had been graphically reminded that the last thing they needed was to draw unwanted attention to themselves. There was a job to be done, and nothing had to get in the way of its successful completion. Least of all the kid's injured pride.

'I told yuh before,' snapped Muldoon, dealing out the cards to his *compadres*. 'Until we get word from Stanton that the guns are ready for shipment, we stay put.'

'And how long is that gonna be?' rasped the kid, sucking on a thin stogie whilst edgily pacing the small room. 'I'm goin' loco stuck here in this dump.'

Muldoon sighed.

'Stanton said that he couldn't siphon off the guns from the armoury until he was able to get rid of the quartermaster sergeant on some legitimate pretext.'

'And when's that gonna be?'

'Should be any day now,' said Muldoon, struggling to keep a cool head. 'Just take it easy. Don't be so impatient. Another few days and we'll all be in the money. Them Cheyenne will pay anything we ask for those new repeaters. In pure gold as well. Ain't that worth waitin' for?' He levelled a dark frown on the young tearaway, willing him to back off.

Soon as this caper was over and the guns had been sold to the Cheyenne, he intended lighting out for California.

Alone.

Sure, the kid was a mean gunhand,

but he was too erratic, a loose cannon and totally unpredictable.

But Kid Striker was not satisfied, and had no intention of 'taking it easy'.

'I'm sick of just hangin' around,' he voiced loudly. 'It's drivin' me crazy.'

'Read a book,' suggested a scrawny runt, adding with a taut sneer. 'That is if'n you got the learnin'.'

Coyote Bill Bristow had acquired his nickname due to a high-pitched nasal twang, an unfortunate abnormality that had earned one chortling wit who had thought it a highly amusing joke, a knife in the brisket. But the name had stuck. Over time, however, Bowman had come to tolerate his sobriquet, even relishing the fact that he had a nickname.

Striker gave a rancid snarl and knocked the proffered tome from Bowman's outstretched hand.

'So what yuh figurin' to do?' rasped Muldoon.

'I'm goin' into town. And none of you jaspers had better try stoppin' me.' His right hand hovered menacingly above the ivory butt of his .44. The icy glower challenged any of his associates to disagree.

A taut atmosphere heavy with menace hung over the group of outlaws.

Muldoon met the Kid's leery gaze evenly. He didn't want to lose face with his new confederates, but neither did he want a showdown that would likely end in terminal gunplay.

He turned to a hefty guy who boasted a rough-hewn face chiselled from pure granite.

'You go with him, Rocky,' he said flatly, holding the kid's insolent leer with a even regard, 'And make sure he don't get into trouble.' Rocky Maddox merely nodded, then stood up looking towards the kid. His own hard look invited the kid to make an issue of the boss's ruling.

Striker gave an arrogant shrug, swung on his heel and strutted outside.

'And I want you back here before sundown,' shouted Muldoon, intent on having the last word.

The gang boss smiled to himself. It had been a close run thing but he had maintained his standing.

⋆ ⋆ ⋆

Following the return of Swooping Owl to the bosom of her family, both Ben and Jericho were anxious to hit the trail. Tribal protocol, however, demanded that Lone Dog celebrate the return of his youngest daughter with a feast at which her two rescuers were to be the guests of honour.

The celebration in the Pawnee camp went on for two days. Only on the morning of the third day were the two partners at last able to make their farewells and depart. Though not before Lone Dog had been fully acquainted with the threatening actions proposed by the Cheyenne.

Ben's departure from the Indian encampment was tinged with regret. During his stay he had become ever more beguiled, enthralled by the simple life style of his hosts. Swooping Owl had played a prominent role in ensuring that when their current task was completed he would most assuredly return.

Although Ben had known the Indian princess for only the briefest of periods, he knew that his relationship with her was more than mere infatuation. Their leave-taking was formal and stilted, as prescribed by tribal etiquette, and therefore all the more disheartening. Would he ever see her again? All he could do now was fervently pray that this would not be their final meeting.

But that would depend on how he and Jericho managed to handle the dangerous task they had set themselves.

Now it was even more vital that they emerged unscathed and on top.

★　★　★

Saratoga was a small town comprising little more than a single main street of log shacks with barely a lick of paint between them. It had grown up to service the discovery of silver in the nearby hills. Unfortunately, the actual delivery of paydirt had not lived up to initial expectations. Only a couple of small mines were still in operation, providing their owners with barely enough lucre to survive.

It was now the influx of cattle-ranching into the Sweetwater Valley that was keeping the town alive.

Nudging their mounts down the dusty street, both men anxiously scanned every passing face. Not that they could have recognized their quarry. All they had to go on were the somewhat vague descriptions passed on by Bull Ferris before he croaked. Few bystanders gave them more than a cursory glance. Just another pair of drifters passing through.

The two travellers dismounted before a saloon sporting the bizarre image of a bright-yellow rooster above the door, tied off and dusted themselves down. At one time there had been half a dozen such establishments serving the needs of the mining community. This was the only one left.

They entered separately so as not to draw unwelcome attention to themselves. Ben immediately angled towards a free table at the rear of the long narrow room whilst Jackson ordered their drinks at the bar. Ben had chosen a spot in the shadows so that they could observe the comings and goings of the clientele without themselves being subject to any scrutiny.

They could be here for a while.

An hour later Ben was dealing out a game of solitaire when he felt a nudge in his ribs. He looked up and followed Jackson's fixed gaze.

Two men had just entered the Yellow Rooster. It was the younger jasper who caught their attention. A cocksure braggart, vain and full of boastful swagger, bellied up to the bar. He slammed a bunched fist down calling for a bottle of whiskey.

'And none of that rot-gut hooch you

serve the yokels.'

The defiant slur echoed around the room.

The barman gave the speaker a tight frown but held his peace. He was used to brash young hardcases who thought they could take on the world. Most of them were soon brought to heel. Just so long as the kid didn't cause trouble, he would take his money same as anyone else's.

Rocky Maddox tensed. His furtive gaze swept the room, noting the unwanted attention the kid was attracting. He was a seasoned outlaw who had always managed to stay one step ahead of the law by maintaining a low profile. It didn't bode well, his having to wet-nurse this reckless asshole.

Clutching the bottle, Maddox ushered the young gunnie over to the end of the bar.

'Hush up that durned gob of yourn,' he rasped throatily. 'The last thing the boss needs is a loudmouth puppy like you puttin' the kibosh on our plans.'

'Who you callin' a puppy?' growled a sullen Kid Striker, his hand dropping to the low-slung gun on his hip.

'Just keep yer lip buttoned,' hissed Maddox, anxious to placate the feisty youth. 'Let's just have us a quiet drink with no trouble.'

The older man's attempt to calm his lively companion appeared to succeed. Striker muttered a few garbled imprecations; something about being accorded the respect he deserved as a more senior member of the gang. Maddox raised his hands in acceptance. He was only too willing to concur. Pouring his unwanted sidekick a drink, he affected a forced smile then raised his own glass to the success of their forthcoming enterprise.

They clinked glasses. Rocky Maddox heaved a muted sigh of relief.

'That must be the one calling hisself Kid Striker,' whispered Jackson, instinctively pulling his hat down even though the kid had never set eyes on him. It was Ben Wallace who needed to keep his face hidden. 'Ain't never seen hair that red afore. Almost looks as if he's on fire.'

'The other guy must be a new member of the gang taken on to replace the one you put away.' There was a hint of venom in Ben's acidic comment as he rose to his feet. He drew his gun and checked the loading.

'What yuh a-doin' of, boy?' asked a worried Jericho Jackson, grabbing at his sleeve.

'I'm going to make him spill the beans once and for all,' snarled Ben, his piercing gaze arrowing towards the two outlaws.

'Ain't you got no sense, boy?'

'Uh?' grunted Ben, a puzzled frown creasing his chiselled features.

'We let 'em drink up, then follow them to the hideout.' Jackson paused, waiting for the penny to drop. 'That way we catch the whole gang in one fell swoop.'

Ben sat down. His face softened as he realized the sagacity of his astute partner's logic.

'How come you always have the right answers, old-timer?' He grinned sheepishly.

Jackson tapped his angular snout with a perceptive wink at his partner.

'Maybe 'cos I bin around for a coon's age.' He smirked. 'Got rid of all my mistakes early on in life. That way you tend to live longer. Jump in head first and you're like to end up on Boot Hill afore your time.'

'That's good advice.'

'You listen to old Jericho Jackson and you won't go far wrong.'

12

Smoke Out

It was another two hours before the pair of outlaws decided to call it a day. Or rather Rocky Maddox did. The kid was becoming a mite too verbose, snarling at anybody who inadvertently bumped into him.

Maddox hustled him outside and on to his horse before any damage could be done. The kid was incapable of any spirited resistance. In fact, he was so drunk that the older man had to tie him to his saddle.

Their return to the gang's hideout was slow and protracted, thus enabling Ben and Jericho to follow at a distance without any difficulty.

They reined up behind some rocks overlooking the front of the cabin. The big jasper known as Rocky hauled the carrot-headed drunk down off his horse, then prodded him towards the cabin door. Once inside, Muldoon's displeasure was unbounded. It could even be heard by the two pursuers.

They grinned at one another.

The virulent harangue was muted and incoherent, but there was no doubt who was on the receiving end. Nor did Rocky Maddox escape the brutal ear-bashing for allowing it to happen.

What now concerned Ben was how to take the gang out. Here they were, stuck out in the open with Muldoon and his roughnecks in the cabin. They needed an angle, a means of gaining the upper hand.

But what?

As usual, it was the wily buffalo-hunter who proposed the answer to their dilemma. It was so simple. He pointed to the wisps of smoke drifting up from the metal stovepipe chimney atop the cabin roof.

The cabin backed on to a jumble of rocks.

'If I sneak around to them rocks,' explained Jackson eagerly, his blue eyes crisp and revitalized, 'I can easily step on to the roof. Then all I have to do is stuff a rag down the chimney, blocking off the smoke.'

'And there's only one way out,' said Ben, quickly catching the old-timer's drift.

'You got it, son.' Jackson nodded. 'It'll force 'em out. And like as not they'll be coughin' their guts up. It'll give us the edge.'

'Then we can pick them off,' rasped Ben venomously. 'Giving them the chance to surrender first,' he added with mocking asperity.

'Of course,' Jackson agreed with a smirk. 'I allus give the lowest of varmints an even break. Keeps my conscience clear for the hereafter, like.'

'But don't forget,' Ben reminded his partner, 'I want Muldoon alive. That critter has a heap of explaining to do.'

Jackson nodded.

Affecting a solemn demeanour, they

shook hands. What they were about to embark upon was no Sunday-school picnic. Both recognized that their joint quest was fast approaching its climax, and they were under no illusions as to the dangers involved.

'Let's get to it then.' Ben hooked out the prized Winchester from its saddle boot and levered a round into the breech. Clutching his own long cherished Sharps 'Big Fifty', Jericho Jackson gave his young *compadre* a tight smile before ducking behind a nearby boulder. Bent low, he scurried across a patch of open ground to the relative safety of cover on the far side.

With a practised eye, Ben followed his partner's progress as the old buffalo-hunter circled carefully around behind the cabin. The last thing he wanted was any harm to come to this old guy whom he had come to regard almost as a father figure.

It was a further fifteen minutes before a thatch of grey hair gingerly poked above the cabin's roof-top.

Jackson raised a hand to indicate he was in position, but didn't wait for any acknowledgement from Ben. The younger man would not want to risk exposing his position.

Tense and keyed up like an over-strung banjo, Ben watched hawk-eyed as Jackson stuffed a pile of wadding into the narrow chimney. Immediately, the smoke was cut off. It would not be long now.

Raised voices and a bout of raucous coughing soon followed.

The cabin door was thrown open and two men emerged encased in a cloud of smoke. The first was a skinny critter followed by Kid Striker.

Ben was ready and all fired up.

'Throw down your weapons and surrender. Or fill your hands, you sons of bitches,' he yelled standing out in the open, the Winchester pulled tightly into his right hip. 'This is the end of the line.'

Momentarily stunned at this unexpected challenge to their freedom, both outlaws just stared agog at the raw-boned man facing them. Then, as one, they grabbed for the holstered shooting-irons on their hips. Without appearing to move, Ben levered off five shots in as many seconds from the Winchester.

Being to the fore Coyote Bill was struck by all five in the neck and upper body. A fountain of red spurted from a ruptured carotid artery. Throwing up his arms, he uttered a choked gurgle and collapsed in a heap.

Youth and the instinct to survive enabled Striker instantly to shrug off the effects of the alcohol he had consumed. He palmed and fanned the Colt Frontier at the threatening appari-tion vaguely perceived through the swirling tendrils of smoke.

Only one struck its target. It was only a nick on the left thigh. But the searing pain was a sufficient inducement to encourage Ben to seek shelter among a nearby cluster of boulders. From there he quickly cut his opponent down with a rapid volley that knocked Striker back against the thick cabin wall. The kid's face creased in agony. For a full minute, he hung there, arms splayed out as if he'd been crucified. Then he sank to his knees and fell forward on to his face, leaving a dark smear of red behind.

Clouds of acrid smoke continued to billow from the cabin forcing a third man to rush outside. After witnessing the gruesome finale of his confederates' demise, Rocky Maddox was taking no undue risks. Coughing and holding a red bandanna to his face, he dashed outside and threw himself behind the water-trough.

From there, he began peppering the scanty cover behind which Ben was cowering. The ex-army officer was unable to move. If he raised his head more than a fraction, Maddox would easily blow it off his shoulders. Sooner rather than later, the outlaw was bound to hit something.

That was when Jericho Jackson

decided it was time for him to take part in the action.

Unfortunately, he could not see Maddox from his position on the cabin roof. The outlaw was concealed beneath the front overhang of the veranda. Sliding catlike down the back of the roof timbers, not an easy task for a buffalo-hunter well past his prime, he none the less managed to drop silently to the ground at the rear of the cabin.

Breathing heavily, he scuttled round the side, gingerly approaching the outlaw's exposed back. Clutched in his hands, Old Hannah waited expectantly. But good fortune was not looking over the old guy's shoulder. Perhaps age was catching up. Or maybe it was Old Nick wanting to even the score. No more than five paces behind the outlaw, he stumbled, twisting his ankle on an unseen rock.

It was enough to warn Rocky Maddox that he was not alone.

He leapt to his feet spinning in a whirl of dust. Discarding his rifle, the outlaw slapped leather and palmed his Smith & Wesson Schofield, triggering and firing two quick shots at the looming threat. The first whipped Jackson's hat from his head, but the second found a more solid target in the form of the old guy's rib cage.

Jackson cried out and pulled up short in his tracks. Old Hannah fell from his grasp as the old-timer staggered back a pace. Maddox uttered a manic shriek of rage, aiming the pistol for the killing shot.

The revolver's hammer never fell.

Two shots echoed across the smoke-blackened clearing. Deep and sonorous, they originated from the barrel of a 'One-in-a-thousand' Winchester.

Maddox emitted a choking gasp, eyes glassing over as his life rapidly ebbed away.

Much as Ben wanted to sprint across the open clearing in front of the cabin, he knew that Polkadot Charlie was still inside, although he was arriving at the conclusion that even a slippery cardsharp like him couldn't survive in the smoke-filled atmosphere for much longer.

He must either be unconscious or dead. But that didn't begin to add up. Why would the varmint allow himself to just keel over with not even a shot fired in retaliation? Ben scratched his head in thought.

Then, like a herd of charging buffalo, it struck him. A dark cast played across his saturnine features. Maybe the slippery cuss had found an escape route. The miners who worked from the cabin might easily have dug a subterranean passage to link up with the diggings.

That had to be the answer.

Tentatively, he stood up revealing his position. Beads of sweat trickled down his neck. If that bastard was in the cabin, here was presented the gold-plated opportunity to dispatch his antagonist to meet his maker.

Not a sound, apart from a faint moan coming from the wounded buffalo-hunter.

Ben dashed across the clearing. After ensuring that the outlaws he had gunned down were indeed headed for the final round-up, he quickly checked the cabin. As he had surmised, it was empty. And there, in the middle of the floor, was an open trapdoor revealing the hidden escape route.

Back outside, Ben climbed on to the roof and removed the wadding from the chimney. Once the smoke had dispersed, he carefully lifted his wounded *compadre* and carried him into the cabin. He laid him down on one of the bunk-beds.

'Your gonna . . . have to do the . . . business this time,' mumbled the old-timer, his leathery visage creased in pain. 'That slug is still inside . . . and it hurts like the devil.' His breathing was shallow and laboured. The bullet must have badly chewed his guts into ribbons.

'I ain't no sawbones, Jericho,' muttered Ben shaking his head and feeling decidedly helpless. 'Maybe I should head for town and find someone to come out here and see to you.'

'There ain't no time fer that,' croaked Jackson, clutching at his partner. 'I'll tell yuh . . . what to . . . do.'

His eyes flickered briefly, emphasizing their crystalline shade of blue. Summoning his last vestige of strength, he raised himself on to one elbow. But the effort was too much, his injuries too severe. As he slumped back his contorted features assumed a wan pallor. Then the eyes glazed over, closing for the last time as life expired from the shattered old frame.

Jericho Jackson had skinned his last buffalo.

A single teardrop etched a path down Ben Wallace's face. His head was bowed in abject sorrow, stunned at the loss of his old partner. He hadn't known Jericho Jackson for long, but it felt as if a part of his very being had been lost. The old buffalo-hunter had become much more than just a trail buddy.

For five minutes he couldn't move,

total inertia having taken over his torpid body.

Then the doleful expression hardened, the strained features twisted into a blunt mask of retribution. Muldoon and his mysterious army contact would pay dearly for this day's work.

13

Going Underground

Ben covered the still form with a blanket, whispered a few solemn words in tribute, then went outside. He humped the three corpses inside the cabin, then peered around in search of some coal-oil. After finding a large tin in a cupboard, he doused the entire cabin with the contents, both inside and out.

It would be a fitting send-off for Jericho Jackson. At the back of Ben's mind was the thought that it would also serve to erase the bodies of the men he had killed. He struck a match and applied the flame to a pair of torch brands, one of which he slung into the furthermost corner of the room. Ben had no intention of joining the souls of the recently departed on their journey to the hereafter.

Ensuring that the cabin was well alight, he ducked down the ladder into the subterranean passage, pulling the trapdoor shut behind him.

Then he set his mind to the grim task of chasing down his quarry. And like a hungry mountain lion, his pursuit would be dogged and persistent.

The tunnel was narrow and constricted, the uneven floor littered with stones. In places, pit-props had been erected to support the workings. but most of these were now rotten and threatened to give way at the slightest disturbance. Ben's faltering progress was slow and measured, to ensure that he avoided any such mishap. He was not helped by the Stygian gloom that was barely penetrated by the flaming coal-oil torch.

He vowed that once out of this fetid warren, never again would he grumble about life on the surface. The question passed through his swimming brain as to how anybody could willingly spend their life scrabbling about in this umbrous world of perpetual night. Not even the lure of precious metals and the rewards on offer could ever be a sufficient enticement for an outdoorsman like Ben ever again to venture underground.

Moisture dripped from the low roof, forming pools of water, some of which were over two feet deep. In no time he was soaked to the skin and wondering when this nightmare would ever reach its finale.

All he could do was stumble onwards, hoping that his torment would eventually run its course.

And so it came to pass.

After what seemed like half a lifetime, he sensed the blackness beginning to lighten. Then, on rounding the next bend, a tiny window of light a hundred yards ahead informed him that his appalling experience was coming to an end. In the cavernous obscurity of the mine, time had lost its meaning. Ben found it impossible to estimate how long he had been incarcerated in the bowels of the earth. All he knew was that at long last the forbidding trek was over.

He rushed forward. And that was almost his undoing. In the headlong dash to bathe in the light of day, his shoulder struck one of the delicate uprights. Creaking and groaning, the rotted timbers threatened to give way.

Panic at the thought of being buried alive lent impetus to his fervent desire to escape. Disquieting growls, as if some primeval beast had been awakened from its slumbers, pursued him along the final section of the tunnel.

Luckily, it was the roof to Ben's rear that collapsed.

Just in the nick of time he propelled himself out into the open, enveloped within a surging miasma of dust and loose stones. The banshee holler of ruptured timbers and crashing rock hammered at his eardrums as he stumbled away from the shattered mine entrance.

Staring back at the chaotic mêlée of boulders, a potent sigh of relief escaped from between clenched teeth as he realized that he had got out unscathed. He sucked in deep lungfuls of fresh air. Never had the dry static heat been so welcome.

The mine entrance was on a ledge some hundred feet above a steep-sided canyon. Acclivitous bluffs of fractured sandstone stretched away into the distance, fingers of rock thrusting out of the sandy floor and poking angrily at the azure sky overhead. It was a bleak terrain, occasional splashes of green clashing with the lurid orange rock where stunted juniper and chollah cactus had managed to secure a toehold.

Shading his eyes against the sun's harsh glare, Ben desperately scanned the landscape, searching for the slightest hint that Muldoon was within reach. His tired body tensed as dust devils chasing each other down the narrow rift gave the illusion of a galloping horse.

All too soon the truth was revealed.

The canyon was empty.

If the gambler had passed this way, doubtless he had secreted a horse at this end of the mine-level beforehand for just such an eventuality. Ben was on foot with no chance of continuing the pursuit. His shoulders drooped as the reality of his situation struck home.

His mouth, dry and rough, felt like sandpaper. A rasping tongue was the painful reminder that in the rush to vacate the cabin he had foolishly overlooked that vital necessity, water. The spring was on the far side of the rocky spur, which was clearly the reason the miners had chosen to erect the cabin there in the first place.

Disconsolate, a sombre mood of melancholia crept over the ex-cavalry officer. He sank down, back against the rock wall, feeling completely impotent; unable either to continue the pursuit of Polkadot Charlie Muldoon, or to retrace his steps. The burning of the cabin and its grim contents had thwarted that choice of action. And the collapsed mine ensured that that line of retreat was also barred.

At some point Ben realized the necessity of having to find a route above the canyon wall leading back to the remains of the cabin where the horses were tethered.

The blistering heat radiating down from a cloudless azure firmament should have been a fillip, an incentive to get moving. But the recent near-death experience had completely sapped his energy. A lethargic torpor gripped his muscles. Watery eyes flickered as the sandman took over.

★　★　★

Three hours later Ben surfaced once more. His tongue was swollen like a hunk of tough saddle-leather. He rubbed his eyes. They felt gritty and sore. Then he tried shaking the lassitude from stiff muscles. Sucking on a round pebble supposedly would help to stem the gnawing thirst that gripped his body. Whoever voiced that opinion was either a liar or a darned fool. All it did for Ben was chafe the dry skin of his mouth.

If he didn't find water soon, he'd be a goner for sure.

Lengthening shadows of late afternoon played across the austere landscape of Snaggletooth Canyon. Contrasting tones of light and dark had mellowed the harsh glare as the sun dipped away towards the western horizon.

But it was the movement along the canyon bottom about a mile away that caught Ben's attention and brought him stumbling to his feet. Etched starkly against the eastern wall, he could clearly see a group of riders heading across his line of vision.

And from their manner and self-assured bearing, he could tell they were Indians. But from which tribe? Cheyenne, and he would be literally in dead trouble. All thoughts of his isolated predicament were forgotten under this new threat. He scuttled behind some nearby cover and ducked down, his whole body tense and edgy.

Another five minutes and he was able to relax.

They were Pawnee and led by a tall, sinewy rider whose head was swathed in an impressive array of eagle-feathers. That must be Lone Dog. Ben removed his hat and frantically waved it to attract their attention. For a brief moment, he thought they had not seen him as the small party continued to maintain a direct course along the canyon floor.

Just as he was about to give up hope, one of them pointed. The head man drew the group of riders to a halt, squinting up towards at the windmilling figure on the ledge above. Ben heaved a thankful sigh as the Indians changed direction, urging their mounts to a gallop. Soon they were zigzagging up the narrow mine-track in single file.

Then his heart skipped a beat. There at the chief's side rode Swooping Owl, a broad smile lighting up her dark satin features. She was clearly pleased to see him. The quixotic feeling was reciprocated fivefold.

Swooping Owl slid effortlessly off a magnificent roan mare and hurried across to greet him. Raven-black hair secured by a beaded headband washed over her slim shoulders. Her pace faltered as she drew closer and took note of Ben's ragged appearance, the dark-red stain on his injured thigh. The radiant smile slipped, tempered by a puzzled frown.

'What has happened?' she queried, the blood draining from her flawless olive complexion. 'And where is buffalo man?'

Ben shook his head unable to meet her anxious gaze. But the meaning was patently obvious.

'He is dead?'

Ben nodded.

'How this happen?' Lone Dog nudged his horse forward. His tone was flat with a barbed edge. Behind and ranged in a semicircle his braves remained astride their wiry mustangs, weapons held at the ready.

Ben forced himself to relive the events of the previous few hours. Concisely he relayed the grim scenario of the battle for the miner's cabin. His narration was briskly delivered and lacking emotion. He knew that the red man looked with scornful disdain on those who succumbed to emotional outbursts. They viewed such displays as a sign of weakness. But the young man could not restrain an ascerbic bite at the finale of his telling of how he had allowed Polkadot Charlie to escape.

That was when Lone Dog gave a prearranged signal. The line of Indian horses parted and the dust-coated figure of that very same polecat was roughly pushed into view. His hands were secured behind his back and blood dripped down his face from a nasty head wound.

Ben immediately guessed that the gang boss must have run slap bang into the Pawnee hunting-party, an assumption that Swooping Owl was able to confirm.

'This the man you talk of?' asked Lone Dog, jabbing his war lance at the cringing figure. Muldoon's normally immaculate vest was torn and the critter was barely recognizable as the cocky gambler of his Leavenworth days.

Ben's mouth twisted into a pitiless grimace. His hooded gaze was filled with loathing.

'That's him all right.'

Unable to contain his anger, he stamped across to the pinioned man and slammed a tight fist into his face. The man reeled under the fierce impact and fell to the ground. None of the surrounding Indians moved. Ben grabbed his jacket and hauled him to his feet. 'Now you're going to tell me the truth,' he rasped.

'I don't know what you mean,' croaked Muldoon, spitting out a mouthful of blood.

'The truth damn you,' howled Ben,

shaking the guy until his teeth rattled. 'Why did you have me driven out of Leavenworth? And then you tried to bushwhack me at Nemaha Gap. You have some explaining to do, mister.'

'You've gotten the wrong man,' asserted Muldoon, forcefully denying any involvement in all of Ben's troubles so far. Then he tried to take the initiative by suggesting that Ben had attacked him and his men without any provocation. And they had only retaliated to protect themselves. 'Seems like it's me that should be having the law come after you. For attacking innocent citizens who are just going about their legitimate business.'

Ben was flabbergasted. His jaw hung slack. He was speechless, completely taken aback by the scheming rat's effrontery.

It was Lone Dog who took the initiative. Turning to Swooping Owl he said, 'Do you know this man?'

She gave a curt nod. 'His name Polkadot Charlie Muldoon. He at Paradise Villa.'

Seated proud and aloof astride a magnificent black stallion, the Pawnee chief made an intimidating figure.

Muldoon had ignored the Indian presence in his desire to escape retribution. Now Lone Dog's cold, menacing stare unnerved the gambler. He knew that redskins had a terrifying way of righting a wrong. And it appeared that Wallace was more than a touch acquainted with this bunch.

'Seize him!' snapped the chief. Instantly half a dozen braves leapt from their horses and grabbed the struggling gambler.

'What yuh gonna do?' he croaked, suddenly overtaken by fearful expectation.

Lone Dog ignored the question.

'This pig has forked tongue, speak plenty lies,' he said quietly whilst slowly and purposefully extracting a huge knife from the heavily ornamented sheath slung round his waist. 'Like poison arrow, it need cutting out.'

Then he walked across the intervening ten yards testing the blade's razor edge. The braves forced Muldoon's mouth ajar. Dreadful squeals of terror elicited derisory grunts from the Indians as the gambler's ogling peepers bulged wide.

Lone Dog was about to stick the glinting steel into the petrified varmint's open maw when a voice rang out across the clearing.

'Wait!'

The deadly blade hovered, inches from the flickering pink tongue. Sweat oozed from every pore of Muldoon's ashen visage.

A buzzard perched on a nearby juniper-branch uttered a manic squawk, annoyed that the gruesome entertainment had been delayed. It was followed by a pregnant silence, the atmosphere charged with menace as Ben strolled casually over to stand before the quaking wreck.

'You have one chance to keep your tongue, Muldoon,' Ben announced, dragging the jigger's petrified gaze to meet his own. 'And that's to reveal the truth, the whole truth and nothing but the truth. Help me nail the bastard who is at the bottom of all this and I'll see you get out of the territory with a full mouth, and a full head of hair.' He wagged a cautionary finger in front of the captive's twitching snout. 'But one false move, and I'll let Lone Dog here make you wish you'd never been born.'

He stood back to let the import of his proposition sink in. 'So what's it to be?'

Muldoon remained tight-lipped, his head had sunk on to his chest.

Momentarily, the quivering gambler was too stunned to realize that he had been thrown a lifeline. He had become resigned to accepting that the removal of his tongue was merely the beginning of what was bound to be death by a thousand agonies.

When Ben shrugged and turned away, he suddenly realized that his life hung by a tenuous thread.

'OK, OK,' he cried, gasping for air. 'I'll do anything you ask. Just keep this red savage away from me.'

'Talk like that isn't going to get you anywhere,' rapped Ben, seeing the grim expression darkening Lone Dog's chiselled countenance, 'except maybe an early grave. You better show some respect to my Pawnee friends, otherwise our deal is off.'

Now that Muldoon realized that the worst of his nightmare was past, some of his old bravado had resurfaced, although he was astute enough to know that you don't look a gift horse in the mouth, otherwise it might just bite your head off.

'Yeah, yeah.' He nodded, gesturing with a conciliatory hand. 'You and the red guys are big buddies. Just keep them away from me, that's all and I'll give the bastard to you on a plate.'

'Now that's just what I want to hear, Charlie,' said Ben sardonically patting the gambler on the cheek. His easygoing smile belied a threat of a fate worse than death should the gambler stray from their tentative agreement.

14

The Trap is Set

Once Polkadot Charlie had ensured that freedom and a fast horse would be the reward for his co-operation in snaring the military renegade, he was more than willing to spill the beans. Ben listened with bated breath as the gambler's astounding revelations unfolded.

It was a story that not even the lurid dime-novelists of the day could have invented.

On discovering that it was Lieutenant Chadwick Stanton who was at the bottom of all his troubles, Ben was completely lost for words; dumbfounded that a fellow officer could have stooped so low. How anyone could betray their own kind by having them cashiered on false charges was beyond his comprehension.

But it was the method by which Stanton had contrived the ignominious disgrace that really stuck in his craw — arranging for the payroll to be robbed where two men were murdered. Then to direct the blame on to the duty officer was the act of a black-hearted coward.

The final straw was learning that Stanton had been promoted to captain and given command of the military stores at Fort Laramie. For a lowlife skunk of his ilk, the opportunities for skulduggery would be endless.

Ben sucked hard on a cigar that had long since gone out. His bloodless lips trembled with suppressed abhorrence that a man he had regarded as more than just a fellow-officer, could at that very moment be surreptitiously commandeering rifles and ammunition for sale to the Cheyenne.

He had to be stopped. And at any cost. Even to forfeiting his own life if that was the price demanded.

Swooping Owl sat cross-legged by his side. She had listened avidly to the blunt discussion between the two white-eyes. Although she had only understood the dialogue in part, it was clear that Bentley Wallace had been sorely wronged. She reached out and held his hand. The action was automatic, a gesture of solidarity. But it was also something more. Ben Wallace imbued her with an inner sense of belonging that she found bewildering yet at the same time strangely exciting.

Ben was more than happy to have her support, even though his stoical expression remained inscrutable.

At the end, silence enfolded the small group. The Indians had squatted down in a half-circle behind their chief and his daughter.

A bleak cast came over Ben's handsome features. The firm set of his jaw told Swooping Owl that only one outcome could be expected.

At first she had argued against his

placing his trust in such a treacherous snake-in-the-grass. Along with her father she had urged that Muldoon be dispatched to burn in the fiery furnace of hell. But Ben had been adamant.

And following much deliberation, he had eventually persuaded them that only with the gambler's help could the real culprit be brought to justice so that Ben could finally clear his name. It would also be a fitting reward for the ultimate sacrifice that Jericho Jackson had made on his behalf.

And so it had been agreed.

To seal the pact, the pipe had been passed round and even Muldoon had deigned to accept a smoke. He rightly considered that until such time as he could light out with his hair intact, discretion would have to be his watchword.

So all that now remained now was for the trap to be set.

* * *

Following some welcome victuals, the two men mounted the pair of Indian mustangs provided by Lone Dog. Muldoon's cayuse had been shot from under him during his pursuit by the Pawnees.

Before leaving, Ben addressed the Indian chief. Something had been bothering him from the moment he had recognized the Pawnee braves in Snaggletooth Canyon.

'How was it that you came upon this varmint?' he asked, jabbing a stiff thumb at his dubious sidekick. 'You are a long way from Rawhide Creek.'

It was Swooping Owl who responded.

'We have to roam much further afield now the buffalo herds are fewer. We saw smoke rising above mountains and came to investigate. This dog was racing his horse like the devil.' Her snarl speared Muldoon with a hate-filled glare. 'Only a man who run from trouble whip a horse like that. We stopped him. Only then did I recognize him as the snake from Paradise Villa.

The one you are seeking.'

'Lucky for me that you were in the neighbourhood.' Ben nodded, brushing a lock of hair off his forehead. 'I was plumb tuckered. Setting fire to the miner's cabin gave Jericho the best send-off he could have wanted. It also brought you here. And gave me the chance to square things with a certain army captain.' He spat out the last word, injecting all the venom he had accumulated since his gratuitous humiliation.

Then he bade farewell to his new *compadres*. Ben's flinty glower softened as he nudged his horse past Swooping Owl. Her brief smile told him to ride a cautious trail, and that she would be awaiting his return.

He and Muldoon were accompanied by a young brave called Two Crows, who was to act as messenger. The Indian had been specifically selected owing to his penchant for the white man's garb. As such he ought to attract less attention at Fort Laramie. Many of his brothers had mocked the brash youngster's choice of apparel, the tribal elders considering it an insult to the old ways.

So far the young brave had resisted all attempts to force him to toe the tribal line, including the addition of a forename. Now the stubborn attitude of Billy Two Crows was receiving the approbation it deserved.

Two Crows smirked at his brothers as he passed, sniffing the air with haughty disregard.

They headed directly for Saratoga.

Ben's plan of action involved the composition of a letter. And the town was the only settlement within fifty miles where writing-implements could be acquired.

Billy Two Crows was to deliver the letter claiming to be a Cheyenne intermediary employed by Muldoon.

Once they had got settled at a table in the local saloon. Ben dictated whilst Muldoon scribbled the missive in his own hand. It read thus:

The Cheyenne are getting restless. They want the guns they was promised pronto. I've gotten together the dough we agreed on. So bring them to the cabin on Highback Mesa where we met up afore. Let Billy Two Crows know when I can expect you. Charlie Muldoon.

PS. Don't panic when you see the cabin. It was burnt down in an accident. Cigars and gunpowder don't mix.

Ben read the missive through carefully. It sounded just right, the language couched in that expected of a gambling man. He sealed it in an envelope and told Muldoon to address it: *For the immediate attention of Captain Chadwick Stanton.*

Even if Two Crows rode flat out, it was a two-day ride to Fort Laramie. Then Stanton would have to make the return trip hauling a buckboard loaded with six boxes of Springfield repeaters plus ammunition. It was now Monday.

Ben could not see the renegade arriving at Highback Mesa before Friday at the earliest. His furtive gaze scanned the saloon. Nobody had taken any notice of the two innocuous strangers.

He shuddered to think on the consequences had he failed to persuade Billy that a saloon was no place for the likes of him.

The Pawnee brave had wanted to accompany them into the saloon in order to partake of the white man's firewater. Ben had bluntly advised against such a course of action. It was a suggestion that Billy was all for ignoring as he made to push Ben aside.

Hastily, Ben had blocked the young brave's path.

'Do you want Lone Dog to learn that one of his most trusted braves has endangered this mission?' he demanded, fixing the youngster with an uncompromising look, frosty as the Arctic wind. 'Go in there now and you will ruin everything. Is that what you want?'

Billy hesitated.

His simple mind found it difficult to accept that many white-eyes still regarded the Indian as a second-class citizen.

'All Two Crows want is to be treated like white man. Have drink at bar.' The petulant grumble was accompanied by a stamping of his feet on the boardwalk.

Ben felt some sympathy for the boy. It wasn't fair, he knew. But that was how things stood at the present time on the Western frontier. He patted the Indian on the shoulder.

'Someday soon, maybe.' Then his voice hardened. 'But not now.'

Billy grumbled some more but his complaints lacked teeth. He didn't want to jeopardize their plans and lose face with the rest of his brothers. Somewhat crestfallen he allowed Ben to usher him quietly to a seat outside the Yellow Rooster.

To soothe the Indian's hurt pride, Ben pulled out a cigar, lit up and handed it to the youngster. Billy's florid countenance split in a beaming grin.

Forgetting all about the desire to taste the white man's firewater, he smugly puffed on the brown tube.

A wry smirk played across Ben's face as he and Muldoon shouldered into the saloon.

'Damn fool Indians,' snorted the gambler, 'Fancy thinkin' they can stand on an equal footing with the likes of us.' Magnanimously included in the cutting retort, Ben ignored the jibe, impatiently directing his associate over to a corner table.

Now he took hold of the letter and stood up, throwing a couple of silver dollars on to the table.

'Get us a bottle while I give the Indian his instructions,' he said.

Muldoon raised his eyebrows in surprise. This was the first time the soldier boy had allowed his guard to slip. It could bode well for the future.

'I'll get us a deck of cards as well.' He gave a smirk. Ben threw him a cynical look. 'Just a friendly game that's all, *Mister* Wallace.' But there was a crafty gleam in the gambler's eye that implied that he would clean this popinjay out if he got the chance.

Swinging on his heel, Ben went outside to find Billy Two Crows happily swathed in a cloud of blue smoke. Gently he removed the half-smoked cigar from between the Indian's thick lips and nipped the end, slotting the butt behind the Indian's ear.

'Time you was hitting the trail,' he whispered, handing over the letter. Then in a deliberately solemn voice intoned, 'Guard it with your life and make certain that only the bluecoat officer named Captain Stanton reads it. No one else.' He paused gripping the Indian firmly by both shoulders and holding the black eyes in a fixed stare. 'And do not forget that you are a Cheyenne. If Stanton has the slightest suspicion that you are a Pawnee, all will be lost. You understand?'

'Ugh!'

Two Crows spat in disgust, his tanned features twisting in an ugly grimace at the thought of having to impersonate his hated enemy. Then he nodded, suitably impressed with the serious nature of his mission.

He was eager to get going. Expressively, he set the eagle-feather in his high-crowned black Stetson at a jaunty angle whilst shrugging deeper into the store-bought jacket. Both were prized possessions that he cherished.

He mounted up, slapped the leather reins against the roan mustang's flanks and galloped off down Saratoga's main drag in a haze of yellow dust.

★ ★ ★

Chadwick Stanton was reclining in the officers' mess. He had been stationed at Fort Laramie for barely a month, having been transferred to the frontier post following his promotion to captain. The unsavoury incident at Fort Leavenworth was all but forgotten, consigned to a dustbin at the back of his mind. He had taken it for granted that his erstwhile colleague, Bentley Wallace, had met a permanent demise at the hands of Polkadot Muldoon and his gang of roughnecks.

A malevolent smirk leered across the glass of French brandy he was sipping. Casually he flicked an invisible spot of dirt from the new tailor-made uniform that had been delivered only that morning. Upon discovering the escalating friction between the Cheyenne and Pawnee, the possibilities of taking advantage of the volatile situation had quickly blossomed in his devious mind.

Security at the fort *vis-à-vis* military equipment was virtually non-existent, a joke even. So Stanton had wired his partner-in-crime, Polkadot Charlie Muldoon, instructing the crafty gambler to get out to Wyoming in double-quick time.

He counted himself fortunate to have been appointed officer in charge of the Fifth Cavalry stores. Consequently, it would be no problem falsifying the delivery invoice and diverting a half-dozen cases of rifles and ammunition to his own use.

All that he would then have to do was choose a night to slip out of the fort unnoticed and make the delivery to Muldoon. Again he smiled, swirling the amber liquor round the glass and savouring its fine aroma.

Life on these remote military outposts might well be far removed from civilization and the fleshpots of Leavenworth, but it certainly had its compensations. If this current scheme worked as well as he expected, Fort Laramie could turn out to be a dream posting.

Just then, a steward approached to inform Stanton that an Indian was asking to see him.

'What does he want?' replied Stanton brusquely.

'Said he had a letter to be delivered personally into the hands of Captain Stanton,' said the steward.

Stanton grunted.

'Tell him to wait outside the stores,' he replied curtly. 'I'll see him in a little while.' Then he settled down once more in his favourite chair to finish his drink. No way was he going to hurry for an Indian. Let the red bastard wait.

Half an hour later he condescended to meet Billy Two Crows. The young Indian was not put out by the apparent rebuff. He was enjoying the sight of a company of horse-soldiers being put through their paces on the parade-ground. It occurred to him that perhaps he could offer his services as a scout. The army were always looking for reliable Indian trackers.

'What do you want, Indian?'

The gruff retort took Billy by surprise. He leapt to his feet, dragging off his hat deferentially. Without speaking he handed over the letter.

Stanton frowned, then managed a tight smile on recognizing Muldoon'a scrawly hand. He tore open the envelope and extracted the brief missive. After digesting the contents, the blunt, hard-boiled expression he reserved for all underlings changed to one of brooding disquiet.

If this were the case, he would have to move faster than he had anticipated.

'Are you one of Polkadot Charlie's boys?' he rapped at the Indian.

The tall rangy Indian assumed an unpenetrable, blank regard.

'Me Cheyenne. Messenger only.'

Billy had deliberately adopted the vernacular of most Indians who came into contact with the white man, mainly to avoid any protracted conversation. He understood the American language more than any of his Pawnee brothers, but recognized that this was not the moment to air such knowledge.

Stanton muttered under his breath. His brow became furrowed in thought For two minutes he said nothing. Billy merely waited.

At last Stanton spoke.

'Tell Muldoon that I will have the goods ready for shipment by tomorrow. He will have them by Friday.' He stared hard at the Indian, reiterating slowly: 'Got that? Friday around noon.'

Billy nodded his head vigorously. Stanton was about to dismiss the Indian when he decided that perhaps a little consideration was needed. Just to ensure that the kid made it back to Highback Mesa, of course. He quickly scribbled out a note and handed it over.

'Here's a chit for some food and supplies for the return journey. Get it from the cookhouse.' He pointed to a long, low building on the far side of the parade-ground.

Billy was delighted. But before he could reply, Stanton was strutting off back to his favourite place, and another brandy.

15

The Final Reckoning

Once Billy Two Crows had departed, Ben judged it prudent to leave Saratoga and return to Highback Mesa at the earliest opportunity. There was no sense in giving his reluctant accomplice the opportunity of hightailing it for pastures unknown — at least not until Muldoon had undertaken his part of the bargain to deliver the bluecoat renegade into his hands.

When they arrived back, he was surprised to see that Lone Dog had established a temporary camp. He had expected the Pawnees to have left. The chief had made it clear that the delivery of much-needed food supplies to the tribal homeland had to be his main priority.

Ben had respected that decision,

although he was more than a little concerned about how he was going to handle the dicey situation of taking out Chad Stanton on his own. Trusting a back-stabbing critter like Polkadot Charlie to toe the line was like stroking the neck of a hungry sidewinder.

So on learning that it was Swooping Owl who had persuaded her father to remain and share the task of preventing the odious gambler from absconding was like music to his ears. His heart skipped a beat as the Indian girl emerged from her tepee.

She smiled coyly, looking more beautiful than ever. Ben returned the gesture, himself a touch reserved.

'It is good to see you, Bentley Wallace,' she said.

Ben merely nodded, his face assuming a faint tinge of red. This was the first time in his life that he had felt tongue-tied, lost for words. Swooping Owl had clearly expected his imminent return and had dressed accordingly.

She looked radiant.

Stepping down from his horse, Ben eventually managed to blurt out:

'I hadn't expected to see you again.'

'Nor I you.'

'Once this business is concluded, perhaps . . . ' The pause brought a lump to his throat. He swallowed awkwardly removing his hat. ' . . . perhaps we could become . . . better acquainted.'

No other female had ever affected him in this manner before. Sure, he had walked out with girls, escorting them to the various social functions arranged by the officers' mess. But they had been the daughters from prestigious military families carefully selected by his parents. Ben had never welcomed their constant interference into his personal life, but had been forced to accept it as the way things were done.

Now he was free of all that false stuffiness. If nothing else, his fall from grace had brought Bentley Wallace into contact with the real world, and real people.

His stilted dialogue, uneven and

unintentionally abrupt on account of nerves, was reciprocated in an equally decorous manner.

Swooping Owl bowed her head in acknowledgement, the black hair glistening in the sunlight. Then she instantly brought her intended paramour firmly back to earth.

'But first we stop sale of guns to Cheyenne. Tribal loyalty must come before own wishes.'

The dewy-eyed moment was over — for the time being.

★   ★   ★

Billy Two Crows reached Highback Mesa late on the Wednesday afternoon. Dark clouds heavy with rain were rearing their ominous heads over the western peaks of the Medicine Bow range. Was the distant rumble of thunder a fateful premonition of things to come? Ben could only hope that such a notion was aimed at Stanton and not himself.

The Indian messenger had ridden hard all the way from Fort Laramie, stopping only for calls of nature. To a young brave of Two Crows' stature, such a feat was nothing. All Pawnee braves were expected to be able to survive in the wilderness from a very young age.

'Did all go well?' asked Ben curtly as he cocked an ear to the west.

'It is so,' replied Two Crows, gratefully accepting a goatskin of water which he drained in a single draught. 'The bluecoat say he will be here Friday at noon.'

Ben nodded. His next remark was delivered in a tone laced with rancorous intent. 'That'll give me time to figure out how to get the drop on him. Cook his goose once and for all.'

His narrowed eyes were already scanning the nearby terrain, seeking out the best place of concealment whilst Muldoon acted out his part as the dutiful gunrunner.

Now that Billy Two Crows had

returned, Lone Dog announced that he would be breaking camp at sunup the following morning. But he offered to leave Two Crows and his brother Grey Bull as back-up. This was a concession that Ben was more than willing to accept.

Much to her father's dismay, Swooping Owl was determined that she also would remain. No amount of parental persuasion and argument could change her mind. She was adamant. Ben Wallace was now her man and she would fight tooth and nail on his behalf.

Ben was in a dilemma. On the one hand he welcomed her zealous support. On the other he was loath to place her in any danger. Bullets would certainly fly. And he had no wish to lose this virtuous angel who had so recently entered his life.

'No Pawnee woman could live with herself if she abandoned her man.' The girl's plain down-to-earth assertion brooked no disagreement.

And thus it was decided.

Chad Stanton had experienced no difficulty commandeering the rifles and ammunition. Their disappearance would be lost amidst the bureaucratic redtape that bedevilled many aspects of military logistics. As a precaution he had exchanged some wooden cases originally containing farm equipment for the rifles.

Like many remote army outposts, Fort Laramie also acted as a local trading centre for the surrounding territory. Any questions raised during a casual inspection could be answered by saying that he had been asked to deliver them personally because the buyer was sick.

He drew the team of four to a halt a half-mile from the steepening gradient at the foot of Highback Mesa.

Hooded eyes suspiciously inspected every nook and cranny in the vicinity. Avidly, they searched for any anomaly that might indicate betrayal. At this critical stage he had no intention of losing out on the promise of a fat wallet. These guns would net him more than he could make in two months, even on a captain's pay.

Chad Stanton had not learned from his previous excesses. Once again he was in debt, numerous creditors already snapping at his heels.

Everything seemed OK.

Muldoon had been right about the cabin. Blackened ribs of the burnt structure stood out against the buff ochre of the rock wall behind.

About to move off, he stopped as a slight movement in front of the ruined cabin attracted his attention. Squinting from beneath a black plainsman's hat, he could just make out a figure signalling him to approach. Even at that distance he recognized the garish vest of his associate.

A smile of satisfaction creased Stanton's angular features.

He flicked the reins urging the team forward.

A plume of dust spiralled into the static air as the sun beat down in relentless fury.

Ben peered at his pocket-watch. Noon on the dot. If nothing else, Stanton had learned punctuality from his military training.

'Get out there and signal him to come in,' snapped Ben to Muldoon. His nervousness was betrayed in the brittle utterence.

Ben had insisted that Swooping Owl keep well back away from any gunplay that might result. The two Indians had secreted themselves at the far side of the shelf behind a huddle of rocks.

It seemed like two lifetimes before the struggling team of four eventually hauled its load up on to the flat breast of Highback Mesa. Stanton cast a wary eye around the clearing before his gaze settled on the hovering figure of Polkadot Charlie.

The army man frowned. Thin blood-less lips compressed into a tight line. Straight away he knew something was wrong. Normally full of swagger and arrogant bluster, the gambler was too quiet. His appearance was dishevelled and shabby. Even from a distance of thirty feet he could smell the guy's fear. And where were the other members of the gang?

Straight away, he knew it was a trap. Muldoon had sold him out.

'I've brought the guns,' Stanton said flatly, trying to conceal any hint of tension. 'Where's the dough?'

'In here,' croaked Muldoon, raising a brown leather bag. His hand was trembling.

Affecting a casual nonchalance, Stanton stepped down off the wagon, but on the far side away from the gambler. He drew his revolver and thumbed back the hammer.

'You're lying,' he snarled. He raised the gun and fired.

Yellow flame belched from the barrel

of the army-issue Remington as two rounds of hot lead pumped out. One of them struck the gambler in the chest. Throwing up his arms, Muldoon screamed and tottered back against a charred hunk of wood.

'Double-crossing skunk,' ranted Stanton waving his pistol. 'This is a set-up. And I'm the sucker who fell for it.'

'No! No!' the gambler howled, clutching at his smashed chest. 'You've gotten it all wrong.'

But he was too late.

Another two shots rang out, this time both found their mark. Muldoon choked on a mouthful of blood, unable to respond. His shattered torso crumpled to the ground and lay still.

That was when the two Indians chose to reveal themselves. Grey Bull raised his bow and loosed an arrow at this devil who intended selling the deadly firesticks to their enemies. The arrow lodged itself in the running-board of the wagon a mere two inches from Stanton's head.

He swung, firing from the hip. His last bullets slammed the redskin back into his brother. That was what saved Billy Two Crows. The young Indian pushed his dead kin aside.

Then, observing the hated bluecoat desperately trying to reload, the youngster dashed across the clearing, tomahawk raised for the final coup. Open-mouthed and bellowing the Pawnee war chant, Billy hurled the deadly blade. Over and over it spun towards its human target, striking the army renegade a stunning blow on the shoulder and glancing off the bone to bury itself in the wagon bed.

The thwack was enough to knock Stanton off balance. Blood poured from the ugly gash. Luckily for him it was only a flesh wound. It hurt like the devil but did not prevent him loading up three cartridges into the revolver. Billy came on, undaunted, fearless and defiant. A wicked-looking knife had replaced the tomahawk.

But sheer cussed bravado was not enough to stop a .36 chunk of lead. Billy stumbled and fell.

That was when a harsh voice stayed the dispatch of any further shots from the gunrunner.

'Remember me, Stanton?'

The renegade ducked down behind the body of the wagon.

For a whole minute Stanton racked his brain, trying to recall that voice. He'd heard it someplace else. Then it came again. This time it was spiked with a potent vehemence that was impossible to ignore, or forget!

'You should have hired someone to do the job properly instead of a scurvy rat like Muldoon.' A pause for effect. 'Now it's too late.'

Those words bouncing off the vertical rock face at the back of the mesa struck the cowering army man smack between the eyes.

Bentley Wallace!

Where in hell's teeth had he sprung from?

The question screamed inside Stanton's befuddled brain. He should have been long since dead.

'Throw your gun out,' hollered Ben from behind a covering boulder. 'This is the end of the line, Stanton. I'm taking you back to prove my innocence and show what a treacherous skunk you really are.' Three shells from the Winchester backed up his demand.

Stanton knew he was in a tight corner. He only had a few shells left. And all it needed was a stray bullet from Wallace's rifle to hit the ammunition box and the whole lot would blow sky high. But he still had one ace up his sleeve.

'OK, Wallace, you win,' he replied, throwing the revolver into the open. 'Don't shoot. I'm coming out.' Then he cautiously stepped from behind the wagon. To his left lay Billy Two Crows. A dark patch covered the whole of the Indian's upper body. He was still breathing, but only just.

Once he could see that Stanton posed

no further threat, Ben showed himself. Eagle-eyed and watchful he joined the renegade, ensuring at all times that the special-edition Winchester was pointing unerringly in his direction.

The turncoat smiled at his hated adversary. The gesture emerged as an ugly grimace. All he had been striving towards now seemed lost. Stanton allowed his arms to drop to his side.

'Keep them arms sky-bound where I can see them,' rapped Ben.

Stanton reluctantly complied.

'You still have to get me back to Fort Laramie, Wallace.'

'I'll rub tobacco juice in my eyes if it means I have to watch over your rotten hide every step of the way,' Ben growled, jabbing the rifle forward. 'After all the strife you've put me through, I'll do anything it takes. There's no way that you can escape justice this time.

'And don't think that with Muldoon dead, there's no proof that you framed me for that payroll robbery.' Ben stood, legs akimbo and smiled, enjoying the moment. He extracted a sealed letter from inside his jacket and held it up. 'He left a signed confession explaining everything — the whole caboodle — how it was you that paid him to do the job.'

This revelation came as a stunning blow to the renegade. Now it was imperative that he expunge this trouble-maker, this ghost from his past, permanently.

'When are you planning to set off?' he asked casually.

'No time like the present. Stick your hands behind your back.'

'You gonna hogtie me then?'

'Damn right!' Ben stepped forward, commandeering a hank of rope from the bed of the wagon. 'I've no intention of giving you the chance to jump me while we're on the move.'

This was what Stanton had been waiting for.

As he lowered his aims, he flexed the fingers of his right hand. Something immediately jumped into his open palm. It was a small up-and-over twin-shot Deringer. The renegade's contorted face twisted into an evil grin. At least Muldoon had had his uses. Concealment of the tiny weapon up his arm had been an afterthought. Never once had he contemplated that it would be put into use.

The gun erupted with a sharp high-pitched crack.

Ben spun under the impact of the small bullet. The rifle slipped from his fingers, his hand jerking upwards towards the injury in his shoulder. It was not fatal, but he had few illusions that the second shot certainly would be.

Stanton quickly stepped forward, straightening his arm to take proper aim.

He uttered a coarse bark of laughter, feverish in its intensity.

'Nobody gets the better of Captain Chadwick Stanton,' he bawled with frantic elation. 'This time I'll make damn certain you don't come back to haunt me.'

That was when the repulsive scowl was wiped from his leering visage. The gun hand wavered and dropped. Stanton wobbled, his legs turning to jelly. Then he tumbled on to his face.

A knife stuck out from his back, blood seeping round the edges of the lethal wound.

Ignoring the dead man, Swooping Owl rushed over to Ben's side. Gently, as if tending a new-born papoose, she cradled his head in her arms.

'Now my father will have to let you stay in my lodge,' she murmured into his ear whilst tenderly stroking his hair.

Ben closed his eyes. A rosy hue bathed the very essence of his being. Life was turning out far better than he could ever have imagined.

We do hope that you have enjoyed reading this large print book.

Did you know that all of our titles are available for purchase?

We publish a wide range of high quality large print books including:
Romances, Mysteries, Classics
General Fiction
Non Fiction and Westerns

Special interest titles available in large print are:
The Little Oxford Dictionary
Music Book, Song Book
Hymn Book, Service Book

Also available from us courtesy of Oxford University Press:
Young Readers' Dictionary
(large print edition)
Young Readers' Thesaurus
(large print edition)

For further information or a free brochure, please contact us at:
Ulverscroft Large Print Books Ltd.,
The Green, Bradgate Road, Anstey,
Leicester, LE7 7FU, England.
Tel: (00 44) **0116 236 4325**
Fax: (00 44) **0116 234 0205**

HAL GRANT'S WAR

Elliot James

When Hal Grant's father was bushwhacked in the street, it was the opening shot of a range war. Wealthy ranchers were determined to rid Lundon County of its sharecroppers and sodbusters eking out an existence in the marginal lands. Hal should have sided with his fellow ranchers, but he did not believe in mob law. He was caught in the middle — and no one was allowed to sit on the fence in a conflagration that was consuming a county . . .

THEY CALLED HIM LIGHTNING

Mark Falcon

A blow to the head had caused him memory loss and temporary blindness. Was he Mike Clancey, the name inscribed on the pocket watch he carried? And the beautiful woman's picture on the inside of the watch — was she his wife? He needed answers. Known as Lightning for his gun skills, riding Thunder, a black gelding, with fair play and talent he would bring a tyrant to justice — but it was a dangerous trail he must follow.

HOMESTEADERS' WAR

Tom Parry

When Wilbur Daniels and his fellow homesteaders are faced with tax demands from the Crossville council, they are up in arms. However, they find support from the ex-sheriff, Luke Tilling, a drunkard who is suffering from a personal tragedy. As bullets begin to fly, a powerful landowner seizes his chance of getting rid of the homesteaders. Not even the beautiful Cordelia can prevent Luke from taking his life in his hands. Will he survive, or will tragedy strike again?

RETURN TO BLACK ROCK

Scott Connor

Despite being innocent, Glenn Price served fifteen years for his father's murder. However, immediately upon his release, he is captured by bounty hunter Randall Nash. Glenn is dragged back to Black Rock, where the townsfolk nearly lynched him before, and soon faces the mob again when the corrupt sheriff charges him with another unjustified allegation of murder. Can Glenn clear his name and find the real killer before the townsfolk invite him to a necktie party?